YAEL

SHE NAILED HIM!

Sometimes It Takes A Woman To Do A Man's Job.

Jacqueline Torres, PhD

First edition 2024

ISBN: 978-1-7340967-6-7

For information on special discounts or for wholesale, please contact Manuscritos Publishing:

manuscritospublishing@cox.net

www.manuscritospublishing.com

authorjacquelinetorres@cox.net

860-748-2906

Other books by the author Jacqueline Torres:

Yael: ¡Una Mujer, Un Clavo, Un Martillo!

Violencia Doméstica y el Sistema Religioso

Los Secretos de Tamar

Dios Tiene Un Plan

Renewing the Spirit of Your Mind

Leadership: Helping Others to Succeed

Power of Change: Reinventing Yourself at any Age

The information presented in this publication is the opinion of the author and is intended only for general informational and educational purposes. The author and publisher waive any representation or warranty, express or implied, with respect to the completeness, accuracy, reliability, suitability or availability of the related information, products, services or graphics in this book for any purpose. The information presented is not intended to diagnose, treat, cure or prevent any condition or disease. Any use of this information is under the sole responsibility of the user.

DEDICATIONS

This book is devoted in particular to women and to people who are taking initiative, emerging from the shadows, and seizing their chance to realize their potential. Women should be confident in their abilities and courageous in serving God in whatever role they find themselves.

It is crucial to recognize that both men and women can be used by God to perform their duties according to His will. Therefore, it is important to avoid any belief that contradicts this principle. Before, during, and after everything was said and done, God was in Yael's tent. Yael's journey was led by a heavenly presence at every stage, revealing a purpose that was beyond her comprehension.

Deborah is praised in the Bible as an inspiration for contemporary women, encouraging them to be strong and knowledgeable without compromising their femininity. Deborah combines feminine traits like elegance, holiness, and humility with assurance and leadership. Deborah's strength, influence, and efficiency were acknowledged. Her example disproved the idea that women couldn't hold positions of authority. She was a well-known and prophetic figure because of the way she combined authority with grace.

It may be difficult for women in some areas to attain positions of expertise and responsibility, which could make it difficult for Deborah's female successors to carry on her legacy. Nevertheless, with God's heavenly direction and purpose, anything is possible. However, the pulpit doesn't seem to be doing much to inspire women to achieve greatness, both intellectually and spiritually, in authentic fellowship with the Holy Spirit. It would be great if more women could be inspired by Deborah and Yael's heroic virtues, even though sermons rarely mention them as an example.

ACKNOWLEDGEMENTS

I would like to express my gratitude to all of the authors and writers who inspired me to write this book. This is a topic of great importance in the contemporary world, where we must recognize and celebrate the contributions of women who are making a difference around the world.

My research and reading on the subject of women, power, and social justice challenged, inspired, and moved me in many ways. I would therefore encourage women in any capacity to engage in teaching and speaking about the courageous women from history, whether they are from the Bible or another historical period.

It is disheartening to observe that even in the present era, women continue to face challenges in asserting their rights. Those in positions of authority seek to revert to the conditions that prevailed in the eighteenth century, when women were denied the right to vote and had to obtain credit through the signature of their husbands. The prevailing opinion was that women were too immature and incapable of independent thought.

To women everywhere, I urge you to persevere in your fight against these injustices. The strength of collective action is a powerful force, and with unity, justice will prevail.

TABLE OF CONTENTS

Jacqueline Torres

INTRODUCTION

As an author and educator, I am always seeking ways to shed light on different books of the Bible by connecting them with current and past trends, resulting in a more comprehensive reading experience. While many authors have written about the Book of Judges, few have explored the story of Yael. Although this is not exhaustive research narrowing the scope has made it more manageable for me and, hopefully, for my readers.

Why did I become interested in Yael? I am interested in the courageous women of the Bible who went against the norm to accomplish a greater mission. Unfortunately, they are often only mentioned for their negative actions on national religious platforms, rather than their positive contributions.

I have always been intrigued by Deborah, the law, the advocate, and the woman (Judges 4:17-24). I have even spoken about her in various national settings. However, despite my knowledge of her and the book of Judges, I overlooked a woman named Yael. As a student of the Bible, I am surprised that I never stopped to ponder about this woman Yael.

That was the start of my research on Yael. I read thirteen books, and each one sparked my curiosity. Certain themes kept recurring, leading me to investigate other sources such as articles, commentaries, and videos from people who shared stories about her. My goal was to gain a deeper understanding of this woman. Along the way, I also studied other Biblical women who shared my passion for social justice.

During my research of information for this book, I found many women in the Bible who made a significant impact on their nations' well-being. However, to avoid oversaturating the story, I decided to focus only on Deborah and Yael. I have already come up with a title for my next book based on my research, but it will not be included in this one. Stay tuned for its release.

The purpose of this book is to promote gender equality and social justice for all, with a focus on empowering women to take a leading role without fear of structural systems. It is designed to encourage all women who teach, preach, and lead to take a bold stand and talk about the women who made a difference in the Bible, rather than just focusing on the contributions made by men. The objective of this study is to facilitate open dialogue about women in the Bible who challenge traditional beliefs and foundational ethical decision-making, yet accomplish great works for their communities.

This book examines the recurring themes and approaches used by authors who have written about women warriors and leaders throughout the history of the Bible. The ongoing debate surrounding gender roles in biblical characters highlights their lasting impact on readers throughout generations. This book presents the main points of various scenarios described in the Book of Judges, which details the activities of twelve judges who are also considered deliverers. However, this book focuses only on the first four judges, Othniel, Ehud, Shamgar, and Deborah.

Throughout history, the question of whether Deborah and Yael set a precedent for women has been asked repeatedly. This story shows how God uses two heroines: Deborah gives the prophecy and Yael carries out the judgment.

I intentionally chose to use the Hebrew name Yael instead of Jael because it has a stronger meaning and purpose. Yael's name derives from the Hebrew verb 'to be useful.' In this book, I will present various scenarios that could have occurred with Yael to encourage readers to think beyond conventional boundaries. I will also draw comparisons with female warriors to contrast them with their male counterparts. The encounter in this book is a dramatic story in three scenes featuring four central characters. It explores the theological beliefs and political commitments between Israel, a faithless but repentant nation, and divine intervention alternating with human action.

The story of Yael and Deborah from the Bible is characterized by gender tension due to Yael's central role in the plot. Some women activists see Yael as a role model, while others see her as radical because she seems to challenge the patriarchy structure. While we can admire the bravery of both women, their violent actions can give cause for concern. Each woman likely believed that sacrificing one person was necessary to save a nation.

The biblical accounts of Deborah and Yael depict a political struggle against a foreign power, culminating in a song of victory. These stories revolve around the issue of a woman's hand and shed light on women's roles in social justice. It is noteworthy that the patriarchal recorders did not mention women by name, indicating their lack of importance in their eyes.

It is important to recognize and appreciate the contributions of women to society. Women exhibit courage and are firmly rooted in reality. They serve as exemplars of moral leadership by demonstrating their talents and virtues. It is important to acknowledge that God is not only the God of men but also the God of women and humanity. Women's worth should not be judged solely by their ability to produce male heirs for their husbands, but also by their ability to accomplish greatness through God's guidance.

Female protagonists like Yael and Deborah are powerful dynamic characters who cannot be lightly brushed aside. The character of these individuals has served as an inspiration even to those who disagree with their actions or beliefs and must reckon with the strength of their character.

The Book of Judges records this period of 20 years to be known as the *dark ages*, during which the Israelites and their wives, mothers, and children were oppressed. Yael provided hope and salvation to the women who dared to be deliverers, and in her memory, Deborah sang a song of blessing.

The women in Scripture are complex figures, just like all of us. They exhibit both fear and courage, bondage and freedom, and are a blend of sin and goodness. These women had to confront patriarchal power, and while some were victims of that power, others used their wisdom to work within the rules of patriarchy to claim their rights and secure their lives. A few even broke all the rules and paid the price. Ultimately, these women are witnesses to faith and justice, persistence and hope, and most of all, restoration to life more abundantly.

The stories of women are the essence of our society. They highlight the increasing trend of poverty affecting women, raise awareness about sexual harassment and exploitation, and call attention to the epidemic of sexual violence and rape. These stories also echo the struggle of women to assert their rights in a patriarchal world. Through their valor and vigor, womanhood brings ancient stories to life and inspires us to fight for their cause.

The patriarchal beliefs and structures of society have relegated women to second-class status, severely limiting their rights and opportunities. In the biblical war story, Deborah and Yael are two empowered women who act as representatives of religious and cultic practices, rather than military commanders. They are God's emissaries who deliver the prophecy and carry out the sentence, playing a major role in the deliverance of the Israelites.

For centuries, the church used the idea that men were created first and women were taken from his rib to deny women access to ministry and authority, confining them to the role of *helper* in the church and family. This belief was based on a subjective interpretation of religious texts and doesn't stand up to scrutiny, particularly when we look at the important roles women played in other parts of the Bible.

Historically, women have had to fight for their survival and inheritance rights to ensure a future for themselves. This has involved challenging the detrimental effects of patriarchal systems that have oppressed and restricted them. Women have challenged the system and brought about changes in laws that prevented them from owning land or inheriting property (Numbers 27:1-11[1]; Law of Inheritance and chapter 36).

---

[1] Then the [five] daughters of Zelophehad the son of Hepher, the son of Gilead, the son of Machir, the son of Manasseh, from the tribes of

Both Deborah and Yael received and interpreted divine communication, making them powerful women who were made even stronger by God's power. The story highlights the important role of women in leadership and their ability to prevail against powerful men in society.

The story of Deborah and Yael in the Bible is an account of powerful women who were empowered by God. In this version of the story, Deborah is portrayed as a counterpart to Moses, a woman who was directly sent by God to call Israel back to the law. An angel appeared to the Israelites and prophesied that a woman would rule and enlighten

Manasseh [who was] the son of Joseph, approached [with a request]. These are the names of his daughters: Mahlah, Noah, Hoglah, Milcah, and Tirzah. [2] They stood before Moses, Eleazar the priest, the leaders, and all the congregation at the doorway of the Tent of Meeting (tabernacle), saying, [3] "Our father died in the wilderness. He was not among those who assembled together against the Lord in the company of Korah, but he died for his own sin [as did all those who rebelled at Kadesh], and he had no sons. [4] Why should the name of our father be removed from his family because he had no son? Give to us a possession (land) among our father's brothers." [5] So Moses brought their case before the Lord. [6] Then the Lord said to Moses, [7] "The request of the daughters of Zelophehad is justified. You shall certainly give them a possession as an inheritance among their father's brothers, and you shall transfer their father's inheritance to them. [8] Further, you shall say to the Israelites, 'If a man dies and has no son, you shall transfer his inheritance to his daughter. [9] If a man has no daughter, then you shall give his inheritance to his brothers. [10] If a man has no brothers, then you shall give his inheritance to his father's brothers. [11] If his father has no brothers, then you shall give his inheritance to his nearest relative in his own family, and he shall take possession of it. It shall be a statute and ordinance to the Israelites, just as the Lord has commanded Moses. (*Amplified Bible ~ AMP*) them for 40 years, the same length of time that Moses led the Israelites through the wilderness (Judges 4:6, 9).

Deborah's story is a testament to the power of wise counsel, strong leadership, and the unwavering belief in divine power. It is a story that continues to inspire and encourage people, especially women, to pursue their dreams and to trust in their abilities.

According to the story, God intervened by opening the heavens and sending down a fierce hailstorm and rain that deflected the aim of the archers, panicked the horses, and mired the chariots in the mud. Deborah's leadership and guidance, along with God's intervention, led to a decisive victory for Barak and his troops.

Deborah was the fourth judge and the only one who is described as serving a judicial function. The judges were in essence tribal heroes or deliverers, whose authority was acknowledged by the people to be from God. They helped to keep Israel from being destroyed or integrated into the surrounding pagan cultures.

The story of Deborah, the inspired judge, continues to resonate with us today. As recorded in the biblical book of Judges 4:1-16 and 5:1-23, Deborah was known for her gifts and abilities, earning respect in her own right. She was a spirited woman, often referred to as a woman of fire. But what's truly remarkable about Deborah is that she was chosen by God in response to cycles of unfaithfulness and repentance by the Israelites, as explained in Judges 2:16-19. As we reflect on Deborah's story, we're reminded of the power of faith and the importance of using our gifts to inspire and lead others.

Deborah was a remarkable woman who was celebrated for her exceptional wisdom in settling disputes, as well as her talents as a military strategist and a leader in a man's world. She was so loved and respected that she was affectionately referred to as *mother in Israel*.

When Barak was uncertain about what to do, Deborah summoned him and informed him of God's plan for his life. She urged him to go to Mount Tabor to lead his men in battle against Sisera, the enemy's general. Despite facing insurmountable odds, including 900 Canaanite chariots made of iron and a fleet of archers, Barak and his soldiers emerged victorious with their swords.

In this narrative, Deborah's role as a prophet is expanded to include the prediction of favorable alignments of celestial bodies for the Israelites in battle. It is important to note that Deborah is not suggesting that the stars acted independently; rather, she employs poetic devices to illustrate that all aspects of creation were aligned to assist the Israelites. The battle of the stars can be understood as a metaphor for God sending a storm to vanquish the enemy and exact divine vengeance. This elevated her to the status of a strategic leader, responsible for directing the forces of Israel. She overshadowed the men in the story, including Barak.

In conclusion, the Bible's story of Deborah and Barak is a powerful testament to the strength and potential of women. It teaches us that God can empower women to lead and inspire their communities, even against the most formidable odds.

On the other hand, Yael is a powerful warrior with a strong physique and muscular strength. Her strength lies in her militant qualities rather than her seductive qualities or status as a warrior woman. She represents a challenge to patriarchal power structures related to gender categories and is not easily defined at a glance.

In the story of Rahab, before the Israelites crossed the Jordan, Joshua sent men to scout out the land. Upon arriving in Jericho, they decided to spend the night at the house of the prostitute Rahab. When Jericho's ruler attempted to capture them, Rahab hid them and then helped them escape through a window, saving their lives (Joshua 2).

The accounts of Rahab and Yael's actions are captivating. Both women were leading their normal lives when political events disrupted their routines. Rahab's house was visited by Israelite men, while Sisera took refuge in Yael's tent.

Each woman faced a critical moment where they had to demonstrate their loyalty. Rahab had to choose between the spies and the king of Jericho, while Yael had to choose between Sisera and Israel.

Despite their loyalties to the Canaanites, both women abandoned them, deceived the Canaanite man, and acted for God and Israel. Their actions had far-reaching implications, and their names are still mentioned centuries later. They showed us that in a crucial moment, our loyalties do not have to be determined by our background, but by our foundational ethical decision-making.

This story highlights how each person has a defining moment when their fate is revealed, and they must prove their worthiness. Rahab and Yael chose to act for God and Israel despite their previous loyalties to the Canaanites. Their actions have historical and cultural significance that impacted the Israelites' destiny. Let us learn from their bravery and commitment, and venture to be loyal to our principles, even in challenging times.

It is noteworthy that in the Bible when a woman performs a good deed using methods typically employed by men, it is often labeled as deception. However, when a man does the same, it is celebrated as heroism. While deception by men is commonplace and accepted, deception by women is only deemed acceptable when her motives are selfless and when she attempts to promote the cause of men to save their reputation. At that point, she is secretly hailed as a heroine, but not praised for too long, so as not to damage men's authority and credibility.

One way to portray female characters as deceitful is by suppressing their motivation, particularly when the deception is linked to women's inferior status and political powerlessness.

During this period, Israel had no king (Judges 19:1; 21:25), and the absence of a stable government led to anarchy a state of disorder due to absence or non-recognition of authority or other controlling systems. God used this as a means of making people aware of the consequences of their arrogance and reliance on themselves.

The Israelites would sin and turn from God, giving in to idolatry, immorality, and suffering at the hands of their pagan enemies. Then, when the people cried out from their oppression and promised to return to faith, God appointed a judge who would be their deliverer.

Acts 13:17-20 ~ *New American Standard Bible (NASB)*

[17] The God of this people Israel chose our fathers and made the people great during their stay in the land of Egypt, and with an uplifted arm He led them out from it. [18] For a period of about forty years He put up with them in the wilderness. [19] When He had destroyed seven nations in the land of Canaan, He distributed their land as an inheritance—all of

which took about 450 years. [20] After these things He gave them judges until Samuel the prophet.

Judges were appointed by God as instruments of divine justice with leadership, administrative, and military authority to rescue His people from idolatry and sin. Twelve judges were appointed to bring salvation to the people. The judges who served were Othniel, Ehud, Shamgar, Deborah, Gideon, Tola, Jair, Jephthah, Ibzan, Elon, Abdon, and Samson. Although most of these judges, excluding Deborah, played more of a deliverer role.

Always be cautious not to assume that God will behave like you. If you possess strength, utilize it for the benefit of others.

NOTES

CHAPTER ONE

CHOSEN AS GOD'S AGENT OF JUSTICE

The texts below weave together selected stories and significant events from the lives and teachings of the Judges, the people of Israel and a woman named Yael. These excerpts are taken from the first five chapters of an ongoing story found in the book of Judges chapters 1-5, New American Standard Bible (NASB).

Judges 1:1-36 ~ Jerusalem Is Captured

[1] Now it came about after the death of Joshua that the sons of Israel inquired of the Lord, saying, "Who shall go up first for us against the Canaanites, to fight against them?" [2] The Lord said, "Judah shall go up; behold, I have handed the land over to him." [3] Then Judah said to his brother Simeon, "Go up with me into the territory allotted me, and let's fight the Canaanites; and I in turn will go with you into the territory allotted you." So Simeon went with him. [4] Judah went up, and the Lord handed over to them the Canaanites and the Perizzites, and they defeated ten thousand men at Bezek. [5] They found Adoni-bezek in Bezek and fought against him, and they defeated the Canaanites and the Perizzites. [6] But Adoni-bezek fled; and they pursued him and caught him, and cut off his thumbs and big toes. [7] And

Adoni-bezek said, "Seventy kings with their thumbs and their big toes cut off used to gather up scraps under my table; as I have done, so God has repaid me." So they brought him to Jerusalem, and he died there.

⁸ Then the sons of Judah fought against Jerusalem and captured it, and struck it with the edge of the sword, and set the city on fire. ⁹ Afterward, the sons of Judah went down to fight against the Canaanites living in the hill country, and in the Negev, and in the lowland. ¹⁰ So Judah went against the Canaanites who lived in Hebron (the name of Hebron was previously Kiriath-arba); and they struck Sheshai, Ahiman, and Talmai.

Capture of Other Cities

¹¹ Then from there he went against the inhabitants of Debir (the name of Debir was previously Kiriath-sepher). ¹² And Caleb said, "Whoever attacks Kiriath-sepher and captures it, I will give him my daughter Achsah as a wife." ¹³ Now Othniel the son of Kenaz, Caleb's younger brother, captured it; so he gave him his daughter Achsah as a wife. ¹⁴ Then it happened that when she came to him, she incited him to ask her father for a field. Then later, she dismounted from her donkey, and Caleb said to her, "What do you want?" ¹⁵ She said to him, "Give me a blessing: since you have given me the land of the Negev, give me springs of water also." So Caleb gave her the upper springs and the lower springs.

[16] Now the descendants of the Kenite, Moses' father-in-law, went up from the city of palms with the sons of Judah, to the wilderness of Judah which is in the south of Arad; and they went and lived with the people. [17] Then Judah went with his brother Simeon, and they struck the Canaanites living in Zephath, and utterly destroyed it. So the name of the city was called Hormah. [18] And Judah took Gaza with its territory, Ashkelon with its territory, and Ekron with its territory. [19] Now the Lord was with Judah, and they took possession of the hill country; but they could not drive out the inhabitants of the valley, because they had iron chariots. [20] Then they gave Hebron to Caleb, as Moses had promised; and he drove out from there the three sons of Anak. [21] But the sons of Benjamin did not drive out the Jebusites who lived in Jerusalem; so the Jebusites have lived with the sons of Benjamin in Jerusalem to this day. [22] Likewise the house of Joseph went up against Bethel, and the Lord was with them. [23] The house of Joseph had men spy out Bethel (the name of the city previously was Luz). [24] And the spies saw a man coming out of the city, and they said to him, "Please show us the entrance to the city, and we will treat you kindly." [25] So he showed them the entrance to the city, and they struck the city with the edge of the sword, but they let the man and all his family go free. [26] Then the man went to the land of the Hittites and built a city, and named it Luz, which is its name to this day.

Places Not Conquered

[27] But Manasseh did not take possession of Beth-shean and its villages, or Taanach and its villages, or the inhabitants of Dor and its villages, or the inhabitants of Ibleam and its villages, or the inhabitants of Megiddo and its villages; so the Canaanites persisted in living in this land. [28] And it came about, when Israel became strong, that they put the Canaanites to forced labor; but they did not drive them out completely.

[29] And Ephraim did not drive out the Canaanites who were living in Gezer; so the Canaanites lived in Gezer among them. [30] Zebulun did not drive out the inhabitants of Kitron, or the inhabitants of Nahalol; so the Canaanites lived among them and became subject to forced labor.

[31] Asher did not drive out the inhabitants of Acco, or the inhabitants of Sidon, or of Ahlab, or of Achzib, Helbah, Aphik, or of Rehob. [32] So the Asherites lived among the Canaanites, the inhabitants of the land; for they did not drive them out.

[33] Naphtali did not drive out the inhabitants of Beth-shemesh, or the inhabitants of Beth-anath, but lived among the Canaanites, the inhabitants of the land; and the inhabitants of Beth-shemesh and Beth-anath became forced labor for them.

34 Then the Amorites forced the sons of Dan into the hill country, for they did not allow them to come down to the valley; 35 yet the Amorites persisted in living on Mount Heres, in Aijalon and Shaalbim; but when the power of the house of Joseph grew strong, they became forced labor. 36 The border of the Amorites ran from the ascent of Akrabbim, from Sela and upward.

Judges 2:1-23 ~ Israel Rebuked

1 Now the angel of the Lord came up from Gilgal to Bochim. And he said, "I brought you up out of Egypt and led you into the land which I have sworn to your fathers; and I said, 'I will never break My covenant with you, 2 and as for you, you shall not make a covenant with the inhabitants of this land; you shall tear down their altars.' But you have not obeyed Me; what is this thing that you have done? 3 Therefore I also said, 'I will not drive them out from you; but they will become like thorns in your sides, and their gods will be a snare to you.'" 4 Now when the angel of the Lord spoke these words to all the sons of Israel, the people raised their voices and wept. 5 So they named that place Bochim; and there they sacrificed to the Lord.

Joshua Dies

6 When Joshua had dismissed the people, the sons of Israel went, each one to his inheritance, to take possession of the land. 7 The people served the Lord all the days of Joshua,

and all the days of the elders who survived Joshua, who had seen all the great work of the Lord which He had done for Israel. [8] Then Joshua the son of Nun, the servant of the Lord, died at the age of 110. [9] And they buried him in the territory of his inheritance in Timnath-heres, in the hill country of Ephraim, north of Mount Gaash. [10] All that generation also were gathered to their fathers; and another generation rose up after them who did not know the Lord, nor even the work which He had done for Israel.

Israel Serves the Baals

[11] Then the sons of Israel did evil in the sight of the Lord and served the Baals, [12] and they abandoned the Lord, the God of their fathers, who had brought them out of the land of Egypt, and they followed other gods from the gods of the peoples who were around them, and bowed down to them; so they provoked the Lord to anger. [13] They abandoned the Lord and served Baal[2] and the Ashtaroth. [14] Then the anger of the Lord burned against Israel, and He handed them over to plunderers, and they plundered them; and He sold them into the hands of their enemies around them, so that they could no longer stand against their enemies. [15] Wherever they went, the hand of the Lord was against them for evil,

---

[2] Baal, god worshipped in many ancient Middle Eastern communities, especially among the Canaanites, who apparently considered him a fertility deity and one of the most important gods in the pantheon. https://www.britannica.com/topic/Baal-ancient-deity

as the Lord had spoken and just as the Lord had sworn to them, so that they were severely distressed.

[16] Then the Lord raised up judges who saved them from the hands of those who plundered them. [17] Yet they did not listen to their judges, for they committed infidelity with other gods and bowed down to them. They turned aside quickly from the way in which their fathers had walked in obeying the commandments of the Lord; they did not do the same as their fathers. [18] And when the Lord raised up judges for them, the Lord was with the judge and saved them from the hand of their enemies all the days of the judge; for the Lord was moved to pity by their groaning because of those who tormented and oppressed them. [19] But it came about, when the judge died, that they would turn back and act more corruptly than their fathers, in following other gods to serve them and bow down to them; they did not abandon their practices or their obstinate ways. [20] So the anger of the Lord burned against Israel, and He said, "Because this nation has violated My covenant which I commanded their fathers, and has not listened to My voice, [21] I in turn will no longer drive out from them any of the nations which Joshua left when he died, [22] in order to test Israel by them, whether they will keep the way of the Lord to walk in it as their fathers did, or not." [23] So the Lord allowed those nations to remain, not driving them out quickly; and He did not hand them over to Joshua.

Brief Analysis of Judges 1 and 2

God is always willing to listen and also to respond with instructions, but will we be willing to follow instructions?

If the men were divinely guided, it is reasonable to conclude that it was God who instructed them.

The covenant made by God has never been broken. It is important to avoid disobedience as it leads to the accumulation of sin upon sin. This is because when you sin against God and forget about Him, you may end up serving other gods.

Joshua who was Moses' successor was careful to review Israel's history with them before he passed away to make sure that they understood that they were to continue to follow in God's way and not turn from Him (Joshua 24:1-16[3]). But then Joshua died and the people forgot their vow to God.

---

[3] Then Joshua gathered all the tribes of Israel to Shechem, and called for the elders of Israel and for their heads and for their judges and for their officers; they presented themselves before God. [2] Joshua said to all the people, "This is what the Lord, the God of Israel, says, 'Your fathers, including Terah, the father of Abraham and the father of Nahor, lived beyond the [Euphrates] River in ancient times; and they served other gods. [3] Then I took your father Abraham from beyond the [Euphrates] River and led him through all the land of Canaan, and multiplied his descendants, and I gave him Isaac. [4] To Isaac I gave Jacob and Esau, and to Esau I gave [the hill country of] Mount Seir to possess; but Jacob and his sons went down to Egypt. [5] Then I sent Moses and Aaron, and I plagued Egypt by what I did in its midst; and afterward I

In these chapters 1 and 2 of Judges, God is specific in answering which of the tribes will first attack the Canaanites and indicates that it is the tribe of Judah. The key word is *attack*. So it indicates that God is involved in the whole process of the attack to ensure that His instructions are followed to the letter. But first, He wants to know if you

brought you out. ⁶ Then I brought your fathers out of Egypt, and you came to the sea; and the Egyptians pursued your fathers with chariots and horsemen to the Red Sea. ⁷ When they cried out to the Lord [for help], He put darkness between you and the Egyptians, and brought the sea upon them and covered them; and your own eyes saw what I did in Egypt. And you lived in the wilderness a long time (forty years). ⁸ Then I brought you into the land of the Amorites who lived on the other side of the Jordan, and they fought with you; and I gave them into your hand, and you took possession of their land and I destroyed them before you. ⁹ Then Balak the son of Zippor, king of Moab, arose and fought against Israel, and he sent and called Balaam the son of Beor to curse you. ¹⁰ But I would not listen to Balaam. Therefore, he had to bless you, so I saved you from Balak's hand. ¹¹ You crossed the Jordan and came to Jericho; and the citizens of Jericho fought against you, as did the Amorite and the Perizzite and the Canaanite and the Hittite and the Girgashite, the Hivite and the Jebusite; and so I gave them into your hand. ¹² I sent the hornet [that is, the terror of you] before you, which drove the two kings of the Amorites out before you; but it was not by your sword or by your bow. ¹³ I gave you a land for which you did not labor, and cities which you did not build, and you live in them; you eat from vineyards and olive groves which you did not plant.' ¹⁴ "Now, therefore, fear the Lord and serve Him in sincerity and in truth; remove the gods which your fathers served on the other side of the [Euphrates] River and in Egypt, and serve the Lord. ¹⁵ If it is unacceptable in your sight to serve the Lord, choose for yourselves this day whom you will serve: whether the gods which your fathers served that were on the other side of the River, or the gods of the Amorites in whose land you live; but as for me and my house, we will serve the Lord." ¹⁶ The people answered, "Far be it from us to abandon (reject) the Lord to serve other gods. (AMP) accept the challenge. Simeon accepted the challenge so they went out together to fight and God helped them. They defeated ten thousand Perizzites and Canaanites, among whom was King Adoni-bezek. During the fight the king had escaped, but they chased and captured him and cut off his thumbs and fat toes. The same king said: God has done to me the same as I did to seventy kings and I had them collecting the crumbs under my table.

The Kenites, who were descendants of Moses' father-in-law along with the tribe of Judah and Simeon, defeated the Canaanites. With the help of God, the tribe of Judah seized the mountainous area, but not the plain, because the inhabitants of that region had iron chariots.

When you focus on your fear and the wrong objective like the chariots of iron you lose sight of the prize!

The other tribes could not conquer the territories and villages assigned to them because the Canaanite inhabitants had iron chariots, although the Israelites were more powerful they decided to force the Canaanites to work for them and live among the tribes. What seemed like a blessing ended up being a curse for the people of Israel!

The time came when God who helped them had to take action on the matter. He sent them an angel with a message letting them know that he took them out of Egypt and brought them into the territory he had promised their ancestors. God had made them a promise that he would give them the land by inheritance and they were to make no deal with the living of that land, but they should destroy their altars of idolatry. But what did the people do? They disobeyed.

While Joshua and the leaders of the land lived the Israelites obeyed the one true God and it was important because those leaders had seen the wonders God had done for the people of Israel. But when Joshua and the Israelites of his time died, only those who knew nothing about the true God or what He had done for Israel remained.

That is why it is important for us who remain and witnessed the greatness that God has done in our lives and generations; must make it a priority to teach this new generation of who God is so that they too will not forget him.

The Israelites stopped worshipping the God of their ancestors and began worshipping the gods of the people who lived around them. This sin made God angry, and he let them attack and steal what they had. He also allowed his enemies to defeat them when they went to fight because God did not go with them and everything went wrong just as God had warned.

God's mercy reaches out to them and He sent them judges to deliver them from those who robbed and attacked them, but they paid no attention to those judges and were not obedient to God, but did as they pleased and worshiped other gods.

When the people complained of their suffering, God pitied them and sent them liberating leaders whom God helped by giving them instructions and saved the Israelite people from their enemies. But when the leader died the Israelites sinned again and stubbornly refused to change their attitude. At first it may seem you have the upper hand until your other gods turn against you and abuse you.

Were the people not communicating with God, or was God not communicating with the people?

Jacqueline Torres

NOTES

CHAPTER TWO

OUT OF THE SHADOWS AND INTO YOUR MOMENT OF DESTINY

Judges 3:1-31 ~ Idolatry Leads to Servitude

[1] Now these are the nations that the Lord left, to test Israel by them (that is, all the Israelites who had not experienced any of the wars of Canaan; [2] only in order that the generations of the sons of Israel might be taught war, those who had not experienced it previously). [3] These nations are: the five governors of the Philistines and all the Canaanites and the Sidonians, and the Hivites who lived on Mount Lebanon, from Mount Baal-hermon as far as Lebo-hamath. [4] They were left to test Israel by them, to find out if they would obey the commandments of the Lord, which He had commanded their fathers through Moses. [5] The sons of Israel lived among the Canaanites, the Hittites, the Amorites, the Perizzites, the Hivites, and the Jebusites; [6] and they took their daughters for themselves as wives, and gave their own daughters to their sons, and served their gods.

[7] So the sons of Israel did what was evil in the sight of the Lord, and they forgot the Lord their God and served the Baals and the Asheroth. [8] Then the anger of the Lord was

kindled against Israel, so that He sold them into the hand of Cushan-rishathaim, king of Mesopotamia; and the sons of Israel served Cushan-rishathaim for eight years.

The First Judge Frees Israel

[9] But the sons of Israel cried out to the Lord, and the Lord raised up a deliverer for the sons of Israel to set them free, Othniel the son of Kenaz, Caleb's younger brother. [10] And the Spirit of the Lord came upon him, and he judged Israel. When he went to war, the Lord handed over to him Cushan-rishathaim king of Mesopotamia, so that he prevailed over Cushan-rishathaim. [11] Then the land was at rest for forty years. And Othniel the son of Kenaz died.

[12] Now the sons of Israel again did evil in the sight of the Lord. So the Lord strengthened Eglon the king of Moab against Israel, because they had done evil in the sight of the Lord. [13] And he gathered to himself the sons of Ammon and Amalek; and he went and defeated Israel, and they took possession of the city of the palm trees. [14] And the sons of Israel served Eglon the king of Moab for eighteen years.

Ehud Kills Eglon

[15] But when the sons of Israel cried out to the Lord, the Lord raised up a deliverer for them, Ehud the son of Gera, the Benjaminite, a left-handed man. And the sons of Israel sent tribute by him to Eglon the king of Moab. [16] Now Ehud made himself a sword which had two edges, a cubit in length, and

he strapped it on his right thigh under his cloak. [17] Then he presented the tribute to Eglon king of Moab. Now Eglon was a very fat man. [18] And it came about, when he had finished presenting the tribute, that Ehud sent away the people who had carried the tribute. [19] But he himself turned back from the idols which were at Gilgal, and said, "I have a secret message for you, O king." And the king said, "Silence!" And all who were attending him left him. [20] Then Ehud came to him while he was sitting in his cool roof chamber alone. And Ehud said, "I have a message from God for you." And he got up from his seat. [21] Then Ehud reached out with his left hand and took the sword from his right thigh, and thrust it into his belly. [22] The hilt of the sword also went in after the blade, and the fat closed over the blade because he did not pull the sword out of his belly; and the refuse came out. [23] Then Ehud went out into the vestibule, and shut the doors of the roof chamber behind him, and locked them.

[24] When he had left, the king's servants came and looked, and behold, the doors of the roof chamber were locked; and they said, "Undoubtedly he is relieving himself in the cool room." [25] So they waited until it would have been shameful to wait longer; but behold, he did not open the doors of the roof chamber. So they took the key and opened them, and behold, their master had fallen to the floor dead.

[26] Now Ehud escaped while they were hesitating, and he passed by the idols and escaped to Seirah. [27] And when he

arrived, he blew the trumpet in the hill country of Ephraim; and the sons of Israel went down with him from the hill country, and he was leading them. [28] Then he said to them, "Pursue them, for the Lord has handed your enemies the Moabites over to you." So they went down after him and took control of the crossing places of the Jordan opposite Moab, and did not allow anyone to cross. [29] They struck and killed about ten thousand Moabites at that time, all robust and valiant men; and no one escaped. [30] So Moab was subdued that day under the hand of Israel. And the land was at rest for eighty years.

Shamgar Saves Israel

[31] Now after him came Shamgar the son of Anath, who struck and killed six hundred Philistines with an oxgoad; and he also saved Israel.

Brief Analysis of Judges 3

Was God involved or not? In these chapters, it is observed that Joshua did not appoint a successor with authority. The reason for this is not explicitly stated. One certainty is that Israel was to educate their children in the commandments of God, despite the absence of a successor to Joshua (Deuteronomy 6:6-7[4]).

---

[4] And you must think constantly about these commandments I am giving you today. [7] You must teach them to your children and talk about

However, after a period of obedience documented in the book of Joshua and following Joshua's death, the tribes of Israel continued their conquest of Canaan. The tribes themselves consulted God through an oracle[5] to determine their next leader, but the nation once again became insubordinate, rebellious, and idolatrous. The Israelites suffered several defeats at the hands of other nations and repeatedly prayed to the Lord for a savior. They failed to drive out seven nations, as the Lord had commanded earlier. The book of Judges chronicles seven instances of rebellion and abandonment of God's sovereignty.

Before many of the Israelites were even born, God purposely left certain Canaanite people to instruct future generations in the ways of war and conquest in the land of Canaan. He leaves five Philistine chiefs to all the Canaanites and other peoples. With these peoples God also tested the Israelites to see if they would obey the orders He had given through Moses, but the Israelites did not obey, but allowed their sons and daughters to marry people from those tribes and worship their pagan gods.

---

them when you are at home or out for a walk; at bedtime and the first thing in the morning.

[5] An oracle is a person or thing considered to provide insight, wise counsel or prophetic predictions, most notably including precognition of the future, inspired by deities. If done through occultic means, it is a form of divination. https://en.wikipedia.org/wiki/Oracle

When you forget God, disobedience leads you into bondage. Sin continues to grow and it shows up in different forms, but the result is the same. God is forced to take his hand away until you cry out to God again and he sends you a deliverer.

In Judges 2:10-19, Scripture describes the cycle of suffering, repentance, and deliverance. It also mentions the first two deliverers, Othniel and Ehud, and how severe suffering can lead a person to turn to God.

Ehud's assignment was: 1) that Israel return to God; 2) kill King Eglon; 3) tear down the idol statues; 4) seize the Jordan River and conquer the territory so that they have 80 years of peace.

God is specific and detailed when giving assignments to avoid confusion about the task at hand. Only God knows what is required to get rid of your enemy, but you have to play the part of obedience.

When God commanded the Israelites to conquer and wipe out the nations who inhabited Canaan, the Israelites did not fully obey Him. Instead, a remnant of the pagan people was left who enticed the Israelites to worship Baal and marry daughters from other nations, further cementing their disloyalty to the Lord (Judges 3:6).

In the book of Judges, we read about the main characters in their role as God's deliverers and the wide variety of unconventional weapons used by various such as Shamgar's oxgoad, Ehud's dagger (Judges 3:16), Yael's hammer (Judges 4:21), Gideon's horns and torches (Judges 7:16), the woman's millstone (Judges 9:53-54[6]), and Samson's donkey jawbone (Judges 15:15). The deliverances of God are rich in detail and captivating, we might not agree with them, but who can question God's ways. But only God knows what is needed to defeat your enemy.

Othniel was the first judge to deliver Israel (Judges 3:7-11). His name originates from Hebrew and means *God's strength* or *God's lion*. The Scriptures describe Othniel's appointment as a judge and leader in Israel, his victory over the king of Mesopotamia, and the subsequent period of peace for Othniel and the Israelites. His judgeship bridged the gap between the leaders of the past and those of his time.

While still mourning Moses' death, Othniel recovered 1,700 legal traditions that the Israelites had forgotten. Othniel restored and reinstated these overlooked teachings and established an academy for Torah study. The families of scribes who lived at Jabez: the Tirathites, Shimeathites, and Sucathites. These are the Kenites who came from

---

[6] But a woman threw an upper millstone on Abimelech's head, crushing his skull. [54] Then he called quickly to the young man, his armor bearer, and said to him, "Draw your sword and kill me, so that it will not be said of me, 'A woman killed him.'" So the young man pierced him through, and he died.

Hammath, the father of the house of Rechab (1 Chronicles 2:55[7]). Othniel's righteousness was so great among his fellow Israelites that God did not hold him accountable for Israel's continued unfaithfulness during his reign.

The story's pattern of reward and punishment is that when the people cry out for help, a deliverer is raised who defeats the oppressors, leading to a period of peace for the people of Israel. The people turned away from the Lord, and as a result, foreign oppressors were allowed to come upon them. This process is repeated throughout the story.

Ehud was the second judge whom the Lord raised up as a deliverer in response to the people's cry for help. Ehud appeared as a name in the Torah and it means *love, pleasant, and united*. This section discusses the story of Ehud in Scripture, which involves a risky assassination of a king and a battle that changed Israel's history for 80 years.

The story emphasizes the removal of a wicked leader and its impact on the nation's history for a generation. It also highlights Ehud's success in achieving freedom, conquering the Jordan River, and killing 10,000 Moabites. Gilgal, an archaeological site in the Jordan Valley, was known for the presence of God. The Moabites kept images of their gods in

---

[7] The house of Rechab is identified with a section of the Kenites who came into Canaan with the Israelites and retained their nomadic habits, and the name of Hemath is mentioned as the patriarch of the whole tribe. https://www.biblicalcyclopedia.com/

Gilgal, which was considered an abomination to God. There's a possibility that Ehud saw images of Chemosh, the Moabite god, as he crossed the Jordan and decided to return to Eglon, who may have believed that Ehud was returning with a message from Chemosh.

Ehud, a person who undertakes great endeavors needs wisdom and courage to execute God's mission. Ehud's calm departure from the murder scene demonstrated his response to divine prompting because he knew who was in control of the events.

During times of war, the Israelites refrained from idolatry, but during times of peace with their enemies, they strayed from God. As with the redemption of Israel from Pharaoh and Egypt, God also redeemed Israel from their bondage under King Eglon when they cried out for help.

Ehud is an exemplar of faithful service to God. His story culminates with him blowing the trumpet on Mount Ephraim and gathering Israel to battle. The story of Ehud takes place 1200 years before the Christian era. While we can't say that Ehud's actions were morally justified, we can assume that he was being influenced by something greater than himself.

Shamgar was the third judge in the Old Testament, responsible for maintaining law and order in the land of Israel. His name means *called, stranger, sword*. It is worth noting that he was the son of Anath, a Pagan goddess, which suggests that Shamgar was one of the foreigners who were regularly being absorbed into Israel during this period. Few people have heard of him, but he was a heroic character who saved Israel by striking down six hundred Philistines with an oxgoad.

During the period of the Judges in the Old Testament, Israel was without a king and the Israelites lacked weapons, living in fear and hiding. Nevertheless, a deliverer emerged to liberate them from their oppressors, demonstrating that God always has the resources at His disposal to accomplish His purposes. Shamgar, a hero who is only briefly mentioned, killed 600 and the weapon he used was an improvised oxgoad, a stick with a sharp iron head on one end used for prodding oxen and a flat chisel on the other end for chipping away dried mud from a plow. He used this tool to save his people. Shamgar got started where he was, used what he had, and did what he could to get the work done. It is important to note that God does not show favoritism. When He has a mission, He will use anyone able and available to fulfill it.

Shamgar, a biblical hero, is one of the most obscure characters in the Bible, mentioned only twice. It is unclear when and where he was born, and the author of Judges does not provide any information about his death. His story is overshadowed by the more important stories of Ehud and Deborah.

Deborah mentions him only once as she describes the historical background that defined the circumstances that made her an important person in the leadership of a nation that is not overtly aggressive but exerts a significant influence on the global political landscape.

Commerce had almost completely halted, and travel had moved from the main highways to smaller and safer byways, the black market was flourishing, and idolatry was preferred to true worship. The Israelites were defenseless and vulnerable to their enemy's assault due to the lack of military training and weapons. This led to an escalation of violence. The Philistines, who had perfected the technology of metal processing, utilized their expertise to make a variety of weapons for warfare (1 Samuel 13:19-23[8]).

The Philistine army instilled fear in the Israelites as they repeatedly attacked them. Shamgar, an Israelite farmer,

---

[8] There were no blacksmiths in the land of Israel in those days. The Philistines wouldn't allow them for fear they would make swords and spears for the Hebrews. [20] So whenever the Israelites needed to sharpen their plowshares, picks, axes, or sickles, they had to take them to a Philistine blacksmith. [21] The charges were as follows: a quarter of an ounce of silver for sharpening a plowshare or a pick, and an eighth of an ounce for sharpening an ax or making the point of an oxgoad. [22] So on the day of the battle none of the people of Israel had a sword or spear, except for Saul and Jonathan. [23] The pass at Micmash had meanwhile been secured by a contingent of the Philistine army. (*New Living Translation ~ NLT*)

felt compelled to act on behalf of his people despite facing an array of disadvantages against the Philistine forces. Firstly, he was a simple farmer and not a trained military soldier. Additionally, he chose to face his adversary alone, believing it to be the best course of action.

Shamgar evaluated the situation, utilized the resources at his disposal, and took action in accordance with his capabilities. Similarly, we should not underestimate our significance, importance, preparedness, or wisdom. These qualities can be used by God for His glory, just as He did with Shamgar.

It is believed that Shamgar's military tactics resemble those of traditional military forces. The fight for freedom was hard but worthwhile. Shamgar led a courageous fight and secured freedom for his people. As a result, he was bestowed the title of judge and Deliverer, and his impact on the history of Israel is regarded as significant.

Like the other judges, Shamgar served as a deliverer for Israel. God's extraordinary purpose during this period of Israel's history is revealed in Judges 3:1-2. The Lord left these foreign nations to test Israel, specifically those who had not experienced the wars in Canaan. The purpose was to teach war to those who had not known it before so that the new generations of Israel might know war. Unfortunately, they failed. Following Shamgar's death,

Israel's sins led to their enslavement under Jabin, a powerful king of Canaan.

To fully understand the significance of this accomplishment, it is important to compare it with other achievements of the same era. Ehud led a successful military campaign against the Moabites, resulting in the elimination of 10,000 Moabites. Barak commanded an army of 10,000 soldiers and defeated an army of 900 chariots and a much larger infantry. Gideon and his 300 men were able to defeat a large army of nomads. Samson once killed 1,000 Philistines using a donkey jawbone, and at the end of his life, he brought down a house on 3,000 Philistines, resulting in his death. When God selects an individual to carry out His will, it is not based on their capacity or ability, but rather on their faithfulness in obedience.

In Judges 3:1, it is stated that these nations were left by the Lord to test Israel. However, the Lord appointed judges to save them. In Numbers 20:16[9], a messenger priest named Phineas announces that the Lord has left the Canaanites as adversaries because Israel failed to tear down the altars of their gods. Israel proceeds to worship these gods, leading to being plundered by its enemies. Once again, they are ultimately saved by judges appointed by the Lord.

---

[9] But when we cried out to the Lord, He heard our voice and sent an angel, and brought us out from Egypt; now behold, we are at Kadesh, a town on the edge of your territory.

Judges 21:25 summarizes the state of the nation of Israel during the time of the Judges sent by God: In those days, there was no king in Israel, and everyone did what was right in their own eyes.

Every Christian is prepared by God to fight a battle. The champions are trained through initiatory encounters to test their abilities.

Jacqueline Torres

NOTES

CHAPTER THREE

FAITHFUL BEFORE AND AFTER, JUST NOT IN BETWEEN!

To fully understand the events of Judges 4 and 5 and its main characters, it is essential to first provide a brief historical context. This will help frame the order of events in this book, including the periods of peace and oppression.

Justice for the People

In Deuteronomy 16:18-20, Moses instructs the people of Israel to appoint judges. He gives the order and Jehoshaphat executes it.

[18] "You shall appoint for yourself judges and officers in all your towns which the LORD your God is giving you, according to your tribes, and they shall judge the people with righteous judgment. [19] You shall not distort justice, you shall not show partiality; and you shall not accept a bribe, because a bribe blinds the eyes of the wise and distorts the words of the righteous. [20] Justice, *and only* justice, you shall pursue, so that you may live and possess the land which the LORD your God is giving you.

Subsequently, Jehoshaphat appointed judges in the Bible (2 Chronicles 19:5-11). The judges of Israel: Othoniel, Ehud, Shamgar, Deborah and Barak, Gideon, Tola, Jair, Jephthah,

Ibzan, Elon, Abdon, Samson, Eli, and Samuel (1 Samuel 1), but these last two judged the entire nation.

The Judges were not a regular succession of governors, but occasional deliverers of different tribes and families, appointed by God to rescue the nation from oppressors, to restore religion, or to administer justice. This is evident in the books of Judges 1-2 and Joshua 16-17. It is worth noting that some cities that were previously declared captured had to be taken over again.

From the judges to the kings, the only time Israel was faithful to God was in war, when they were united in military exploits. From the time of Joshua's death until the establishment of the monarchy in Israel, the judges were the deliverers, guardians, and protectors of Israel. The people suffered when they disobeyed and worshiped other pagan gods. God has many instruments of judgment. God's justice may use one sin, such as Moab's ambition, to punish another, such as Israel's idolatry.

In essence, if you display arrogance, God may allow someone even more arrogant than you to teach you a lesson. This experience can lead you to seek God's forgiveness and restore a godly attitude.

In the Old Testament, the judges were appointed by God to serve as military leaders for the defense of the Israelites in times of external danger. However, these judges only exercised their authority over one or another tribe and never over the entire nation. The judges were appointed as instruments of God's perfect justice and acted as both civil magistrates and military defenders of the nation of Israel. The Hebrew word for judge, shaphat, means *to deliver* or *to rule*.

To provide some brief background, there were two other judges, Eli and Samuel. Both were priests and judges, but Samuel was also a prophet[10]. Their judgeships are described in 1 Samuel 1. They exercised authority over the entire nation until the monarchy was established. The period of the judges ended when Israel demanded a king like other nations.

Eli had been a priest in Israel and a judge for forty years. Eli is best remembered for his blessing on Samuel's mother and for his part in Samuel's first prophecy. Eli had two wicked sons named Hophni and Phineas; they also served in the tabernacle but did not know the Lord (1 Samuel 2:12). It is difficult to fathom the possibility of serving in the tabernacle without any knowledge of the Lord. They violated the Law by keeping and eating meat from the

---

[10] Prophet (because prophet has other definitions outside of the religious context): **Strictly speaking** in religion, a prophet or prophetess is an individual who is regarded as being in contact with a divine being and is said to speak on behalf of that being, serving as an intermediary with humanity by delivering messages or teachings from the supernatural source to other people. The message that the prophet conveys is called a prophecy. https://en.wikipedia.org/wiki/Prophet

sacrifices that were not allocated to them. They also had sex with the women who served at the doorway to the *tent of meeting* (1 Samuel 2:22). The bad behavior of Eli's sons was widely known (1 Samuel 2:24), and the report came back to Eli. When he found out about these things, he rebuked his sons but failed to make them stop, allowing them to continue to profane the tabernacle (1 Samuel 2:25). The tent of meeting, Exodus 33:7-9 ~ Now Moses used to take the tent and pitch it outside the camp, a good distance from the camp, and he called it the tent of meeting. And everyone who sought the Lord would go out to the tent of meeting which was outside the camp. [8] And it came about, whenever Moses went out to the tent, that all the people would arise and stand, each at the entrance of his tent, and gaze after Moses until he entered the tent. [9] Whenever Moses entered the tent, the pillar of cloud would descend and stand at the entrance of the tent; and the Lord would speak with Moses. It's in the tent of meeting where God speaks to you.

God sent Samuel the prophet[11] to Eli with a dire message about his household saying: I will cut short the strength of your priestly house so that no one in it will reach old age. Another more faithful priest would supplant Eli's family line: I will raise up for myself a faithful priest, who will do according to what is in my heart and mind. I will firmly

---

[11] 1 Samuel 3:1-20

establish his priestly house, and they will minister before my anointed one always (1 Samuel 2:35).

Shortly after, the Philistines attacked Israel. Hophni and Phineas, Eli's sons, took the Ark of the Covenant with them to battle, hoping it would protect them. It is unlikely that taking the Ark of the Covenant will result in a favorable outcome for those who do so. This is because God does not operate in such a manner, He rather have obedience than sacrifice. Interestingly, they did not know God, but they wanted to *bribe* Him by taking the Ark of the Covenant with them. You cannot buy God, nor can you sell Him.

However, this evidence suggests that they were unaware of the Lord and it proved that God was not on their side, and the Philistines killed Hophni and Phineas, along with about 30,000 Israelite foot soldiers. The Philistines also captured the Ark of the Covenant. Upon hearing the unfortunate news, Eli fell from his seat, resulting in a broken neck due to his advanced age and weight (1 Samuel 4:3, 10, 17–18).

After making these judgments, God continued to guide His people's leadership even during these challenging times. Samuel became Israel's spiritual leader, serving as judge, priest, and prophet. He marked the transition from the period of judges to the period of kings by anointing both Saul and David as Israel's first two kings. It is noteworthy that Samuel, not God, named his two sons as judges over Israel, and they took bribes and perverted justice (1 Samuel

8:1-3). Ministering to God is not a *business* where you can put those close to you in positions of authority, especially if you've been chosen to carry out God's plan and mission.

A priest's vocation does not guarantee that his or her children will follow in their footsteps. Furthermore, priests cannot simply promote their children to leadership positions within the Church. They must receive clear instructions from God and be prepared to punish those who disobey them. God is highly selective in the individuals He appoints to minister to Him.

In Samuel's situation the elders of Israel approached him and expressed their desire to have a king like the other nations had to judge and rule them. They cited Samuel's old age and his sons' failure to follow in his footsteps, and that his sons' behaviors was deemed unholy. Despite Samuel's warnings, the people were determined to get their own way and ultimately rejected God, choosing a king instead (1 Samuel 8:10-22).

Saul was appointed as the first king of Israel by the prophet Samuel. In 1 Samuel 15:3, God commanded Saul through the prophet Samuel to attack the Amalekites and destroy everything they had without sparing them. However, Saul turned away from following God's orders and disobeyed His commandments.

As a result, the Lord spoke to Samuel expressing regret for appointing Saul as king. Samuel was deeply saddened by this and spent the entire night crying out to the Lord. God's heart was broken by Saul's disobedience. The man who began with humility and submission to God eventually went astray in disobedience. Samuel confronts Saul, saying: As you have rejected the word of the Lord, He has also rejected you as king. Samuel must now execute God's plan.

In **1 Samuel 15:32-34 ~ The Living Bible (TLB)**

[32] Then Samuel said, Bring King Agag to me. Agag arrived all full of smiles, for he thought, Surely the worst is over and I have been spared! [33] But Samuel said, As your sword has killed the sons of many mothers, now your mother shall be childless. And Samuel chopped him in pieces before the Lord at Gilgal. [34] Then Samuel went home to Ramah, and Saul returned to Gibeah.

It is important to distinguish between the anointing and the appointing. While we may be aware of the beginning and the end, it is the middle that requires our attention.

Judges 4:1-24 ~ Deborah and Barak

[1] Then the sons of Israel again did evil in the sight of the Lord, after Ehud died. [2] So the Lord sold them into the hand of Jabin king of Canaan, who reigned in Hazor; and the commander of his army was Sisera, who lived in Harosheth-hagoyim. [3] The sons of Israel cried out to the Lord; for he

had nine hundred iron chariots, and he oppressed the sons of Israel severely for twenty years.

4 Now Deborah, a prophetess, the wife of Lappidoth, was judging Israel at that time. 5 She used to sit under the palm tree of Deborah between Ramah and Bethel in the hill country of Ephraim; and the sons of Israel went up to her for judgment. 6 Now she sent word and summoned Barak the son of Abinoam from Kedesh-naphtali, and said to him, "The Lord, the God of Israel, has indeed commanded, 'Go and march to Mount Tabor, and take with you ten thousand men from the sons of Naphtali and from the sons of Zebulun. 7 I will draw out to you Sisera, the commander of Jabin's army, with his chariots and his many troops to the river Kishon, and I will hand him over to you.'" 8 Then Barak said to her, "If you will go with me, then I will go; but if you will not go with me, I will not go." 9 She said, "I will certainly go with you; however, the fame shall not be yours on the journey that you are about to take, for the Lord will sell Sisera into the hand of a woman." Then Deborah got up and went with Barak to Kedesh. 10 Barak summoned Zebulun and Naphtali to Kedesh, and ten thousand men went up with him; Deborah also went up with him.

11 Now Heber the Kenite had separated himself from the Kenites, from the sons of Hobab the father-in-law of Moses, and had pitched his tent as far away as the oak in Zaanannim, which is near Kedesh.

[12] Then they told Sisera that Barak the son of Abinoam had gone up to Mount Tabor. [13] Sisera summoned all his chariots, nine hundred iron chariots, and all the people who were with him, from Harosheth-hagoyim to the river Kishon. [14] Then Deborah said to Barak, "Arise! For this is the day on which the Lord has handed Sisera over to you; behold, the Lord has gone out before you." So Barak went down from Mount Tabor with ten thousand men following him. [15] And the Lord routed Sisera and all his chariots and all his army with the edge of the sword before Barak; and Sisera got down from his chariot and fled on foot. [16] But Barak pursued the chariots and the army as far as Harosheth-hagoyim, and all the army of Sisera fell by the edge of the sword; not even one was left.

[17] Now Sisera fled on foot to the tent of Jael the wife of Heber the Kenite, because there was peace between Jabin the king of Hazor and the house of Heber the Kenite. [18] And Jael went out to meet Sisera, and said to him, "Turn aside, my master, turn aside to me! Do not be afraid." So he turned aside to her into the tent, and she covered him with a rug. [19] And he said to her, "Please give me a little water to drink, for I am thirsty." So she opened a leather bottle of milk and gave him a drink; then she covered him. [20] And he said to her, "Stand in the doorway of the tent, and it shall be if anyone comes and inquires of you, and says, 'Is there anyone here?' that you shall say, 'No.'" [21] But Jael, Heber's wife, took a tent peg and a hammer in her hand, and went

secretly to him and drove the peg into his temple, and it went through into the ground; for he was sound asleep and exhausted. So he died. [22] And behold, while Barak was pursuing Sisera, Jael came out to meet him and said to him, "Come, and I will show you the man whom you are seeking." So he entered with her, and behold, Sisera was lying dead with the tent peg in his temple.

[23] So God subdued Jabin the king of Canaan on that day before the sons of Israel. [24] And the hand of the sons of Israel pressed harder and harder upon Jabin the king of Canaan, until they had eliminated Jabin the king of Canaan.

Brief Analysis of Judges 4 and 5

While Israel cried out *how long must we wait*; God cried out *how long will you keep sinning*!

Once again, the Israelites have done evil in the sight of the Lord. This time, they were handed over to Jabin, the king of Hazor, and his general, Sisera, who oppressed Israel for 20 years.

In Judges 4:1-24, the powerful stories of Othniel, Ehud, and Deborah unfold. Deborah, appointed by God as a judge, led and guided the people of Israel in upholding righteousness. These judges served as regional leaders, settling disputes, inspiring the people to follow God, and at times, leading battles against their enemies. These narratives offer insights into Israel's political and military landscape, highlighting their faithfulness or disloyalty to God. The text underscores the notion that wicked deeds result in defeat, necessitating deliverance by a godly spirit-filled, anointed, and gifted leader. Deborah received a revelation for a plan of salvation and recognized the paramount importance of acknowledging that regardless of the battle's outcome, God fought for them.

Deborah was a prophetess, community leader, military strategist, poet, judge, and the wife of Lappidoth. She sat under her palm tree in the hill country of Ephraim, where people sought her judgment in settling disputes. Deborah was able to discern and mediate between God and people because of her spiritual gifts. She served as a conduit to God, allowing her to judge both on and off the battlefield. Her gender did not affect her ability to lead in the military. On the contrary, it reinforced the impression of her as a divinely inspired judge who transcended typical gender roles.

Women play a prominent role in the Book of Judges and frequently outperform men. Deborah did not rely on men for her power. As a woman in a male-dominated society, Deborah was justified in initiating war against the Canaanites and recruiting Barak to lead Israel's army. She also participated in the battle herself and exercised her authority for the good of the people, which led to her memorable elevation to public dignity and supreme authority.

Deborah is a judge, and the same term is used to describe Moses (Exodus 18:13-16[12]) and Samuel (1 Samuel 17:6), as well as the judges appointed in each of the tribes of Israel (Deuteronomy 16:18-20[13]), when God chooses you, is to be a representative of God's authority, but when you get it twisted is when you forget who appointed you (Deuteronomy 17:12[14]).

Deborah was elevated by God because of her devotion to keeping the sanctuary bright with fire, making candles with extra thick wicks for her husband to bring to the sanctuary to keep it lit. She was also devoted to Torah study and lived

---

[12] And it came about the next day, that Moses sat to judge the people, and the people stood before Moses from the morning until the evening. [14] Now when Moses' father-in-law saw all that he was doing for the people, he said, "What is this thing that you are doing for the people? Why do you alone sit as judge and all the people stand before you from morning until evening?" [15] Moses said to his father-in-law, "Because the people come to me to inquire of God. [16] When they have a dispute, it comes to me, and I judge between someone and his neighbor and make known the statutes of God and His laws."

[13] "You shall appoint for yourself judges and officers in all your towns which the Lord your God is giving you, according to your tribes, and they shall judge the people with righteous judgment. [19] You shall not distort justice, you shall not show partiality; and you shall not accept a bribe, because a bribe blinds the eyes of the wise and distorts the words of the righteous. [20] Justice, and only justice, you shall pursue, so that you may live and possess the land which the Lord your God is giving you.

[14] But the person who acts insolently by not listening to the priest who stands there to serve the Lord your God, nor to the judge, that person shall die; so you shall eliminate the evil from Israel.

an exemplary life following the law. Deborah's leadership in the rabbinic tradition has received mixed reviews, with some interpreters praising her as a prophet, a wise judge, and a woman of fire, and others suggesting that her title as judge and her leadership in Barak's army may have made her prideful.

Judges 4:1, states that the Israelites sinned again before God, and after the victory song in Judges 5, Judges 6:1 simply reports that the Israelites sinned. After a while, even God gets tired of naming the sin.

In Judges 4:6, God had already spoken to Barak twice before Deborah's second summons. Deborah was used as an agent by the Spirit of God. Her role was to sentence, not to strike, and to command, not to execute. She is a prophetess, a woman who upholds the truth. Deborah's example demonstrates that God is impartial because the two leaders shared a common goal which was to bring glory to God and save Israel.

Deborah requested that Barak bring 10,000 warriors to fight Sisera at the Kishon river. Barak hesitated initially but agreed to go only after Deborah promised to accompany him. Deborah prophesied that the enemy would be defeated by a woman, but it is unclear whether she was referring to herself but later on, we find out who was that woman. The Israelites show surprising fortitude and even govern empires with ability despite being neglected and lacking adequate armor. Nevertheless, Deborah instructed the warriors to engage in battle, assuring them that God would grant them victory. In response to Barak surrendering his leadership to a woman, Deborah accepted the position of leadership, stating that God had given her the rank to lead, not Barak.

Deborah wasn't worried about who was leading because she was more concerned about putting an end to the oppression of her people and just wanted victory for Israel.

Upon seeing Sisera's massive troops, Barak and the Israelites were frightened and considered surrendering. Barak and Deborah were initially shocked but quickly filled with joy because they remembered the prophecy. Barak asked Deborah, the messenger and chosen of God, to accompany him as he did not know when the Lord would grant him success on the battlefield.

Barak believed that victory in battle depended on the presence of God's chosen one. The words spoken to Deborah elevated her status as a female warrior and predicted Sisera's defeat by a woman. Imagine going to war on a mission to destroy your enemy, putting yourself in harm's way, only to be told that someone else will get the victory for killing the enemy, not you?

Deborah accompanies Barak to war and defeats the Canaanites, but the Canaanite general, Sisera, escapes. It was incumbent upon every Israelite who had an opportunity to slay Sisera to be on guard.

When Sisera escaped, Meroz who was within distance could have assisted but he chose not to due to pride. Meroz did not take part in the battle because a woman was leading the charge and had the most authority in the matter. They could not believe that a group of unarmed slaves could achieve such a great victory. The combination of pride and unbelief made them unwilling to follow Deborah into battle. In Judges 5:23, Meroz was cursed by the angel of Jehovah for not helping against Sisera, while Yael was praised for her actions because she accepted the call. It is important to note that pride and unbelief are not praised and are considered signs of weakness and disobedience. When God says *Assemble*, you better assemble!

On Mount Tabor, the prophetess Débora declares God's victory and forecasts Israel's redemption from their enemy, Sisera. Like Moses, Deborah is not a battle commander. Her role is to inspire, predict, and celebrate in victory song, using the power of the Prophetic Word as her weapon.

Although Barak is mentioned as a hero of faith in Hebrews 11:32, his faith relied on Deborah's influence with God rather than his own. He preferred the inspiration of Deborah's visible presence to the invisible but certain help of almighty God.

The Song of Deborah describes how God defeated Canaan through a flash flood that created a swamp of slippery mud, rendering the chariots of iron useless. However, Sisera managed to escape but was eventually defeated. Sisera fled from Deborah and Barak to the tent of Yael, the wife of Heber the Kenite. It is important to note that the Kenites and Jabin the king of Hazor were at peace.

Reflection: Did God intentionally allow Sisera to escape? Did God already know that he would escape? Did He allow it on purpose because He already had a plan in place for the victory? Was God in control?

Jacqueline Torres

NOTES

CHAPTER FOUR

A MISGUIDED SENSE OF HOPE

Sisera was the commander of Jabin's army. He was a Canaanite general who was depicted as a tyrant. His voice was said to bring down walls, his body was beyond description, and it took 900 horses to draw his chariot of iron making his defeat all the more remarkable.

By the age of 30, he had conquered much of the world however, some viewed him as a blasphemer of God and an enemy of Israel. Sisera oppressed and reviled the Israelites, making his death at the hands of a woman, Yael, all the more competent. It is important to note that Sisera was not a victim, but rather the cause of much suffering among the Israelites. Sisera was responsible for many years of oppressive actions.

Sisera sought refuge in the tent of Yael, located among the oak trees that were considered sacred places according to the Hebrew Bible. Yael belonged to an elite priestly Kenite family, and her tent was considered a sanctuary for the fleeing Israelite. The location of the tent near Kedesh is listed as a city of refuge (Joshua 20:7[15]). Sisera made a

---

[15] The following cities were designated as cities of refuge: Kedesh of Galilee, in the hill country of Naphtali; Shechem, in the hill country of

mistake by seeking refuge in the tent of Yael, a woman who was in her tent alone. If her husband had found him there, it could have led to a bloody feud for 20 generations.

After the defeat of his forces, Sisera, an exhausted warrior, becomes vulnerable and in fear for his life. Because of a political connection between Yael's husband and Sisera, he abandons his chariot and flees on foot to Yael's tent.

Yael's portrayal has varied throughout history along with some interpretations depicting her as a true deliverer while others portray her as a deceitful and lustful woman. However, since the 19th century, it has been recognized that her actions were a means of protecting herself and others from the rape that Sisera's mother believed was the right of the victors of war. Yael is often praised for her actions, in contrast to Sisera's mother who eagerly awaits her son's return and the spoils of war, including the captured women.

Sisera's mother, a *spoiled* criminal by association who has become accustomed to her son's return from his military campaigns with numerous female captives is now anticipating his triumphant return, expecting him to emerge from the battlefield with the spoils of victory. Having said that, this expectation was ultimately unfounded and ultimately futile in terms of the well-being of women

Ephraim; and Kiriath-arba (that is, Hebron), in the hill country of Judah. (NLT)

who had been victimized. Sisera's mother expresses a misguided sense of hope, and the absence of a holy and confident expectation of God's providence, as well as a sense of God's guidance and protection, can result in a lack of direction and confusion. She attempts to convince herself that all is well, even as she contemplates the captured spoils of war and refers to women as booty.

She exemplifies an ungodly heart. How shameful are these wishes of a mother for a beloved son, and his officers and soldiers; that a woman of honor and virtue, as we say, could delight her fancy with conceiving the Israelites virgins divided among the conquerors, as their property, to be exposed to their unbridled domineer lust! And that nothing more excellent could be conceived by her trifling mind than to see her son and his attendants and concubines, arrayed in fine garments, wrought by the singular skill and industry of their vanquished enemies. Someone needs to break the news that *Sisera won't be coming home, mother*!

Conversely, the contrasts between Sisera's mother and these two women are striking. Whereas Yael exemplifies the deliverer warrior tradition, Deborah is a multifaceted figure, embodying the roles of mother of Israel, poet, prophet, and judge.

People will rob you of your blessing if you're not careful to stay on task. Don't confuse God's mission with your decision.

CHAPTER FIVE

DELIVERED INTO THE HANDS OF A WOMAN!

In Judges 4, General Barak under the prophecy of Judge Deborah led the Israelite army in a surprise attack against their oppressors, rescuing Israel from slavery. The success of the plan seemed improbable because the army lacked soldiers and weapons and needed divine intervention. Deborah prophesied I will go with you, but you will not receive glory on this journey, for the Lord will deliver Sisera into the hands of a woman. Was Yael the woman referred to in Deborah's prophecy or did Deborah believe it was her? The woman in question was not an unidentified person living among the enemy in the wilderness. God knew who she was for He had appointed her to be the deliverer of Israel.

Judges 4:17-23, highlights the significance of the tent and Heber's wife Yael after the battle. The story clarifies that Heber had a treaty with the Canaanites, which is reasonable given that the Kenites were often blacksmiths. Heber may have positioned his tent near the battle to service the weaponry. Sisera was aware that Heber worked for Jabin the king of Hazor and may have assumed that Heber's wife would be loyal to her husband's ally. Sisera may have sought shelter in Heber's Kenite tent due to their location which was marked as a sacred place and Heber's association with priestly status as a Medianite and his familial connection to Moses' father-in-law Jethro.

Yael was married to Heber, a Kenanite who was descended from Jethro, Moses' father-in-law from the Midianites. Her family were priests, commercial pathfinders, metalworkers, and wanderers who sought work wherever they could find it.

The Kenite tent provided sanctuary and it has been suggested that Kenite and Midianite women played a role in religious and cultic practices. Sisera may have perceived Yael as a priestess. Yael's invitation to Sisera is unusual, as women do not usually invite men into their tents. This invitation would have been considered a violation of hospitality rules in those days. Yael's repeated invitation to *turn aside* meaning come in may imply that she recognizes him and intends to be alone with him in her tent.

In Judges 5:6, it is worth noting that the reference to the days of Yael implies that she was a well-known public figure. Yael is a figure of admiration for her role in the Battle of Mount Tabor, as described in chapters 4 and 5 of the Book of Judges.

For more than twenty years of Yael's adult life, the Israelites were oppressed by King Jabin of the Canaanites. Yael witnessed the destructive cycle of idolatry and judgment that led to the destruction of the land and the acculturation of pagan practices. Yael understands the reasons behind this situation and believes that her people are enduring overwhelming oppression due to Israel's lack of faith and worship of the one true God. Yael believes that if the Israelites humble themselves and turn back to the God of their nation, God will free them from slavery and oppression.

While Heber was in charge of making weapons, Yael's main job was to make tents. This was because traditionally, tents were set up by women and not men. She had become an expert in all phases of tent-making, including spinning goat hair, weaving, and setting up and taking down tents during travel. Yael's expertise in this area was crucial to the success of their journeys. According to tradition, the woman and her husband would have had separate tents, which would have doubled her workload, efforts, and required skills.

Yael's ability to use a tent pin and hammer to secure stakes into the desert ground was useful in General Sisera's deception and execution. Her experience living in a tent and developing these skills demonstrates her resourcefulness. Yael pitched her tent under a sacred oak tree in Zaananim, consecrating it as holy ground. This historic site is located in Nephtali, a land designated for fleeing individuals from the 12 tribes of Israel. After the defeat of the Canaanites, Sisera sought refuge in Yael's tent, family, and land.

Heber, whose name means *ally*, contracts himself out to the Canaanite army led by General Sisera for weapon-making. He travels north from Judah to Canaan, taking Yael with him. Heber assumes that the Canaanites have a military advantage, but it is important to remember that God is on Israel's side. Unfortunately, Heber falls into the same trap as the nation of Israel and enjoys the riches and spoils of the land, compromising his integrity and beliefs in the process.

To protect his interests, Heber may have informed General Sisera of Barak's battle plan and was likely rewarded with a commission to build 900 iron chariots. Heber and Yael lived safely and prosperously under a ratified peace treaty between themselves and General Sisera. During the battle between Canaan and Israel, severe weather conditions affected the Canaanite army, hindering their vision and making it difficult for their chariots to move. This was seen as a sign of divine intervention in favor of Israel. Similar to the Egyptians' experience in the parting of the Red Sea, the Canaanites are defeated, leaving Sisera as the sole survivor. He escapes with his life, running to Yael's tent of asylum, assured of his safety and protection at the hands of his friends. Sisera believes he is safe upon entering Yael's tent, which is considered a refuge on sacred ground.

Upon receiving news of the Israelites' victory over the Canaanites, Yael may have felt compelled to align herself with the winning side for her safety. Yael was considered an ally by Sisera, and after his army was destroyed, he sought refuge in her tent. She welcomed and nourished him, gaining his trust before ultimately killing him.

It is important to note that Sisera entered Yael's tent, not her husband's tent. Heber is noticeably absent, probably killed in battle. The ancient laws of hospitality in the Middle East were very strict. Once a guest is formally invited into a home, they are to be protected and cared for, even at the expense of everyone else in the house. This included the possibility of the woman of the house being given to the guest of honor for his pleasure.

The responsibility of offering traditional hospitality fell solely on the head of the household. Yael, however, provided refuge to a fleeing enemy general, which is not considered traditional hospitality. Therefore, Yael cannot be accused of failing to provide hospitality. Nevertheless, it would have damaged Yael's reputation if Sisera had been alone with her. Understandably, her innocence was in danger of being violated.

Sisera assumed he would find a welcome place in Yael's tent because she was probably not an Israelite. However, the Kenites also worshipped the God of Israel and were familiar with the laws of God. Yael, being a true Hebrew woman at heart, betrayed him.

Did Yael violate standards of hospitality or act as God's agent of justice? Was she simply trying to protect herself against the approaching Israelite army, who were hot on Sisera's heels? Maybe she was worried that Sisera was ready to claim her as a spoil of war or hold her hostage? Why did Sisera approach Yael's tent? Was he seeking refuge from a political ally, or did he not have a better option at the moment? Or was it that God was directing the scene?

Yael the non-Israelite heroine is portrayed as the instrument of God's deliverance. This seems to align with the proverb in Exodus 23:22, which states that if one listens carefully to God's commands and obeys them, He will be an enemy to their enemies and oppose those who oppose them. The heroine's actions ultimately advance the cause of the Israelites. During times of war, women were frequently subjected to rape and captivity as a reward for victory.

If Sisera had been killed by a man instead of Yael, would that have been more acceptable to the Israelite communities of that time?

In Yael's story, gender reversals begin with the irony of Sisera addressing her in a condescending masculine form and assuming that only men are significant. The reason behind Sisera's request for her to *Stand at the door of the tent and if anybody comes and asks if there is anyone here, say No*, remains unclear. Yael's answer, *NO*, proves prescient as it saves her from becoming a raped and murdered woman.

Yael's gender and male politics put her in a vulnerable position. Heber was not at home that day as he was preparing the chariot force for battle. Yael's actions were driven by survival instincts. Yael's decision to kill Sisera was an act of self-defense. This parallel suggests that Yael is portrayed as a heroine for Israel by behaving like an Israelite hero. When she sees Barak, she offers to show him *the man whom you seek* (Judges 4:22).

Take a look at how Yael and Sisera are portrayed in the story. Yael is a strong woman, but because of the way society was set up at the time, she was vulnerable to abuse. For example, the change of a male enemy warrior into a woman who would have been taken prisoner and raped shows how women were seen as possessions. Another example of this is Judges 5:27, which talks about how female captives were seen as treasures to be won by the captors.

Yael's actions were heroic and a testament to her sense of duty. It is not fair to criticize her for breaching hospitality when she was chosen as an agent of God's justice, thus it is unfair to condemn her for showing a lack of hospitality. Justice must be carried out in God's world by all means required. The foundation of God's kingdom is joy, peace, and justice in the Holy Spirit. In God's world, justice must be served by any means necessary. God's kingdom is built on justice, peace, and joy in the Holy Spirit (Romans 14:17[16]).

If Yael had not sheltered Sisera, he would likely have killed her or taken her captive. By preventing Sisera from escaping, she helped Barak achieve victory, fulfilled God's will, and earned great honor for delivering the oppressed people of Israel from the fearsome general.

Judges 4:17-22; 5:24-27, describes the encounter between Yael the Kenite and Sisera, commander of the army of Jabin king of Hazor. Sisera imposes himself on Yael and makes demands in her tent. The scene where Yael kills Sisera is a reversal of rape, where the rapist becomes the victim.

Yael, a Kenite woman, initially integrated geographically and subsequently ethnically into the tribe of Judah and cooperated with them to defeat Sisera, a seasoned warrior. Despite Sisera's superior strength, Yael's success was due to her faith and commitment to the right cause (Judges 1:16; 4:11, 17; 1 Samuel 15:6; 1 Chronicles 2:55).

When a foreign woman chooses to embrace Israelite society and religion and demonstrates a serious commitment to her new community, her acceptance is guaranteed. Additionally, her foreignness enhances the impact of her deed.

---

[16] For the kingdom of God is not eating and drinking, but righteousness and peace and joy in the Holy Spirit.

In Judges 4:9, it is prophesied that the Lord will sell Sisera into the hand of a woman, and this prophecy is fulfilled when Sisera becomes Yael's captive. Yael's perspective is not presented, leaving her vulnerable. However, she completed the task at hand and delivered Israel from oppression, deserving of Deborah's blessing. Yael was chosen to execute divine judgment.

Yael was a woman of virtue who acted with righteous anger against her enemies. This act humbled the Canaanite king Jabin until the Israelites were able to destroy him.

In the story, we read that the enemy was in Yael's tent. The practices of hospitality were insignificant in comparison to the potential dangers that she might encounter. Yael used a hammer to drive a nail into Sisera's temples. The mind is widely regarded as the seat of authority and power, and it is where our will is rooted. It is important to submit our will to God's will and ask for the Holy Spirit to purify and cleanse our minds (Proverbs 23:7[17] and 2 Corinthians 10:4-5[18]).

The period of oppression lasted for twenty years, but after Yael defeated Sisera there was a forty-year period of peace.

---

[17] For as he thinks within himself, so he is. He says to you, "Eat and drink!" But his heart is not with you.

[18] For the weapons of our warfare are not of the flesh, but divinely powerful for the destruction of fortresses. [5] We are destroying arguments and all arrogance raised against the knowledge of God, and we are taking every thought captive to the obedience of Christ.

The relevant scriptures are Judges 4:1-5:31, 1 Samuel 12:11, and Hebrews 11:32.

The Song of Deborah recounts the great victory and it is a great example of how God has a divine plan for every encounter in our lives (Judges 5:1-31).

The ancient song *Blessed be Yael* depicts women warriors without any ambivalence towards their actions. It is important to note that this is not always the case in stories about women warriors. The song does not provide any information on how Yael came to be near the battlefield or why she acted on behalf of Israel. Yael's appearance is not described, and Sisera does not react to her in any way other than as a source of rescue for him. It is important to note that the Bible does not condemn Yael's actions; instead, she is to be celebrated, as we will emphasize in a later chapter. Yael acted under the divine will and fulfilled a divine prophecy. It is unclear whether she felt a divine call directly from God or through God's prophet Deborah. However, God permitted Sisera to be captured by a woman, thereby fulfilling the prophecy.

According to Judges 5:31, Israel experienced 40 years of peace. Yael envisioned herself fulfilling her duty and believed that she was called by God to serve His people. Yael's loyalty differed from that of her husband, and she sympathized with the side that was favored by God.

It is noteworthy that Yael, the guerrilla warrior, informs Barak that she has the man he seeks. Deborah the Judge sings a victory song in honor of Yael. Two women, one mission: Peace for Israel!

Reflection: Was God controlling all of Yael's actions in the tent? Did Deborah know that it wasn't her? Did God not reveal that secret in the prophecy? Why not? Would that have made Deborah not want to go on that mission because she wasn't going to get the victory? How would you have reacted? Would you have said, it is not your job?

NOTES

CHAPTER SIX

THE PROPHECY. THE COMMAND.

THE KILLING.

Hypothesis

This chapter offers a fresh perspective on the encounter between Yael and Sisera, proposing that Yael may not have acted alone but under the guidance of a divine messenger.

God is capable of utilizing any resources to achieve His objectives, and on occasion, He may employ individuals or methods that are not immediately apparent as being ideal. This is because God is not constrained by the limitations of human perception, and we often impose such limitations upon Him. It is crucial to recognize that the trajectory of one's life is not fixed; one's role and circumstances may shift unexpectedly. In a given period, one might be appointed by God to assume a leadership role, while in another, one may be called to serve in a more passive capacity.

In ancient Near Eastern cultures, the interpretation of dreams was regarded as the principal mode of communication between humanity and the spiritual realm. This aligns with the widely held belief that *God is in control*, promoting thought-provoking creativity and underscoring the idea that human actions do not influence God's decisions in His mission.

For instance, Numbers 12:3-8 ~ Now the man Moses was very humble, more than any person who was on the face of the earth.) **4** And the LORD suddenly said to Moses and to Aaron and Miriam, "You three go out to the tent of meeting." So the three of them went out. **5** Then the LORD came down in a pillar of cloud and stood at the entrance of the tent; and He called Aaron and Miriam. When they had both come forward, **6** He said, "Now hear My words: If there is a prophet among you, I, the LORD, will make Myself known to him in a vision. I will speak with him in a dream. **7** *It is* not this way *for* My servant Moses; He is faithful in all My household; **8** With him I speak mouth to mouth, That is, openly, and not using mysterious language, And he beholds the form of the LORD. So why were you not afraid To speak against My servant, against Moses?"

And in Job 33:15-17 ~ In a dream, a vision of the night, when deep sleep falls on people, while they slumber in their beds, **16** Then He opens the ears of people, and horrifies them with warnings, **17** So that He may turn a person away from bad conduct, and keep a man from pride.

Elaborating deeper on this hypotheses, the term *theophany* comes from the Greek and is used for the words *God* and *Appearance*, and it refers to instances in which God reveals himself to humans in a visible form. Examples of theophanies in the Bible include the burning bush, pillars of clouds and fire, Mount Sinai, and appearances to prophets such as Isaiah, Ezekiel, Joseph, David, Daniel, and many others. The New Testament also includes theophanies to Joseph and Mary. In Genesis 15[19], Abraham experiences a theophany while in a state of altered consciousness during sleep, and Adam also experiences a theophany in a similar state in Genesis 2:21, So the Lord God caused a deep sleep to fall upon the man, and he slept; then He took one of his ribs and closed up the flesh at that place.

The account of Deborah and Barak's conflict with the Canaanites depicts God as an active participant who guides the narrative and determines its outcome. The divine intervention takes place in history when God's messengers appear and signs are witnessed. While it is commonly said that God is in control, it could be argued that Yael's cultic and divination practices are also subject to God's sovereignty.

Reflection: Did David kill Goliath because of the stones or was it due to divine intervention from God? Was God controlling all of Yael's actions in the tent? Did Moses part the Red Sea or did God intervene? Who sent the plagues to Egypt? Who made rain brimstone and fire on Sodom and

---

[19] After these things the word of the Lord came to Abram in a vision, saying, "Do not fear, Abram, I am a shield to you; Your reward shall be very great."

Gomorrah? Did Joseph get sold into slavery because of his brother's or did God have a greater plan for him becoming governor of Egypt?

The Bible acknowledges dreams as a valid means of divine communication and dream interpretation as divinely inspired (Genesis 40:8[20]; Daniel 2:25-31[21]; Jacob's vision (Genesis 28:11- 13[22]), Salomon's dream in Gibeon (1 Kings

---

[20] And they said to him, "We have had a dream, and there is no one to interpret it." Then Joseph said to them, "Do interpretations not belong to God? Tell it to me, please."

[21] Then Arioch hurriedly brought Daniel into the king's presence and spoke to him as follows: "I have found a man among the exiles from Judah who can make the interpretation known to the king!" [26] The king said to Daniel, whose name was Belteshazzar, "Are you able to make known to me the dream which I have seen and its interpretation?" [27] Daniel answered before the king and said, "As for the secret about which the king has inquired, neither wise men, sorcerers, soothsayer priests, nor diviners are able to declare it to the king. [28] However, there is a God in heaven who reveals secrets, and He has made known to King Nebuchadnezzar what will take place in the latter days. This was your dream and the visions in your mind while on your bed. [29] As for you, O king, while on your bed your thoughts turned to what would take place in the future; and He who reveals secrets has made known to you what will take place. [30] But as for me, this secret has not been revealed to me for any wisdom residing in me more than in any other living person, but for the purpose of making the interpretation known to the king, and that you may understand the thoughts of your mind. [31] "You, O king, were watching and behold, there was a single great statue; that statue, which was large and of extraordinary radiance, was standing in front of you, and its appearance was awesome.

[22] And he happened upon a particular place and spent the night there, because the sun had set; and he took one of the stones of the place and made it a support for his head, and lay down in that place. [12] And he had a dream, and behold, a ladder was set up on the earth with its top reaching to heaven; and behold, the angels of God were ascending and

3:3-5, 15[23]). Joseph functioned as a dream interpreter and considered a diviner in Egypt (Genesis 40:5-19; 41:1-32), the Plagues (Exodus 7:14; 12:36) and Sodom and Gomorrah (Genesis 19:24-25).

The narratives of Yael and Sisera, Deborah and Barak share similar themes. In Judges chapters 4 and 5, we find the story of two military leaders who seek advice from cultic mediators or diviners and are told that victory over the Canaanites will be achieved by killing their enemy.

After being defeated in the war against Israel, Sisera abandoned his chariot and fled the battlefield. His soldiers retreated towards their city in search of shelter and protection (Judges 4:15). In contrast, Sisera fled on foot to avoid being recognized and because of the peace treaty between Jabin king of Hazor and the Kenites, he sought

---

descending on it. [13] Then behold, the Lord was standing above it and said, "I am the Lord, the God of your father Abraham and the God of Isaac; the land on which you lie I will give to you and to your descendants.

[23] Now Solomon loved the Lord, walking in the statutes of his father David, except that he was sacrificing and burning incense on the high places. [4] And the king went to Gibeon to sacrifice there, because that was the great high place; Solomon offered a thousand burnt offerings on that altar. [5] In Gibeon the Lord appeared to Solomon in a dream at night; and God said, "Ask what you wish Me to give you." [15] Then Solomon awoke, and behold, it was a dream. And he came to Jerusalem and stood before the ark of the covenant of the Lord, and offered burnt offerings and made peace offerings, and held a feast for all his servants.

sanctuary in the tent of Yael the Kenite which was in the territory of Israel (Judges 4:17).

In the ancient Near East, it was considered unusual for a woman to leave her tent and greet a man who was not a member of her family. Yael left the tent to meet Sisera and later on Barak. Yael's deliberate choice to engage with these men while remaining within the sacred boundaries of the tent carries significant symbolic weight, underscoring the importance of her actions.

There's a possibility that Yael held a position as a cultic functionary and public figure, which granted her greater freedom of speech and movement than the average woman. As an individual who likely played a role in her community, she was probably accustomed to receiving visitors in her tent.

The tent of Yael was designed like a temple with an open courtyard and a distinctive cultic function. This space was regarded as sacred and accessible only to cultic functionaries and priests (Exodus 27:9-19; Leviticus 6:9; 1 Kings 8:64).

Yael's tent is located in a sacred place where she consults the gods. Yael is presented as a recognized figure who practices the art of divination and interprets dreams to predict the future. Yael uses the elements of an offering of a *cultic meal* prepared by the medium, similar to the encounter in 1 Samuel 28:3-8[24].

If we accept this interpretation, the story is similar to that of King Saul and the Medium of Endor. In his desperation, since he was able to escape, he was curious about his fate. Sisera sought the help of Yael, a diviner and cult practitioner, to learn about his future. Sisera realized that his defeat was not caused by the small Israelite army, but rather by the God of Israel who had determined the outcome of the battle (Judges 5:20-21).

The setting, atmosphere, imagery, and dialogues point to a different picture, not of a chance encounter of a defeated general seeking shelter with a woman in front of her tent, but of a military leader seeking an audience with a female cultic intermediary to learn about his future fate. Similar to the encounter between King Saul, the medium of Endor, and Samuel's spirit on the eve of Saul's final battle with the Philistines (1 Samuel 28:9-25).

---

[24] Now Samuel was dead, and all Israel had mourned for him and buried him in his own town of Ramah. Saul had expelled the mediums and spiritists from the land. 4 The Philistines assembled and came and set up camp at Shunem, while Saul gathered all Israel and set up camp at Gilboa. 5 When Saul saw the Philistine army, he was afraid; terror filled his heart. 6 He inquired of the Lord, but the Lord did not answer him by dreams or Urim or prophets. 7 Saul then said to his attendants, "Find me a woman who is a medium, so I may go and inquire of her." "There is one in Endor," they said. 8 So Saul disguised himself, putting on other clothes, and at night he and two men went to the woman. "Consult a spirit for me," he said, "and bring up for me the one I name."

When individuals are confronted with a challenging problem, they may find it beneficial to take a temporary break from attempting to resolve it. This period of rest and reflection, known as an incubation period, can provide a much-needed opportunity for creative thinking and problem-solving.

The practice of incubation, or sleeping in a sacred place and making ritual offerings, was believed to facilitate divine messages or dreams and was thought to be widely practiced. This practice was often associated with the seeking of guidance or insight from the divine. However, the interpretation of divine revelations through dreams, known as divination, required the expertise of intermediaries, as not everyone possessed the ability to decipher dreams and apparitions.

Another practice was necromancy, which also required techniques to conjure and converse with the dead. In Mesopotamia, a seer, often a woman diviner, would sit near the head of the dreamer to explain, interpret, and translate the dream.

When angels appeared to ordinary people, it was thought that they would be amazed, and more surprised when the divine angels would give them revelation knowledge. Occasionally, divine messengers would say they don't need to bow down, but that they must stand humbly before the presence of God (Genesis 18:1-3, 8,[25]; Exodus 17:6[26]; 33:10[27]; Ezekiel 2:1[28]).

In Ephesians 6:14-15 ~ Stand firm therefore, having belted your waist with truth, and having put on the breastplate of righteousness, [15] and having strapped on your feet the preparation of the gospel of peace. The feet symbolize preparedness and readiness to accept the call and walk in God's ways, the way of faith and sharing the Gospel. Is God telling you that He has come to you to make you a servant and a witness of what He has done and will do? Now, stand up in humble acceptance.

In the Pentateuch, the phrase *the door of the tent* refers to a place of special importance where God appears and

---

[25] Now the Lord appeared to Abraham by the oaks of Mamre, while he was sitting at the tent door in the heat of the day. [2] When he raised his eyes and looked, behold, three men were standing opposite him; and when he saw them, he ran from the tent door to meet them and bowed down to the ground, and said, "My Lord, if now I have found favor in Your sight, please do not pass Your servant by.[8] He took curds and milk and the calf which he had prepared, and set it before them; and he was standing by them under the tree as they ate.

[26] Behold, I will stand before you there on the rock at Horeb; and you shall strike the rock, and water will come out of it, so that the people may drink." And Moses did so in the sight of the elders of Israel.

[27] When all the people saw the pillar of cloud standing at the entrance of the tent, all the people would stand and worship, each at the entrance of his tent.

[28] Then He said to me, "Son of man, stand on your feet, and I will speak with you."

speaks (Exodus 33:9-10; Numbers 12:5-6[29]; Deuteronomy 31:15[30]). Yael's command to *deny the presence of a man* in her tent leads to the most crucial moment of the encounter, marking the transformation in her behavior.

Yael and Sisera are communicating back and forth in this scene and suddenly Sisera, the commander of the Canaanite army, appears to have fallen asleep. Was there a third person in the tent who was giving orders to Yael?

The sequence of events in the tent, which is part of the divine revelation, contrasts with the cultic practices and divination. Is this the exact moment when the messenger of the prophecy enters and speaks with Yael? Was it Sisera who gave the order to deny the presence of a man or was it the Divine Messenger? Was it really Yael who did the killing or was she just left holding the weapon?

In Judges 4:18, Yael reassures Sisera not to fear, despite his reputation as a warrior who takes women as spoils of battle (Judges 5:28-30). The phrase *Do Not Fear* resonates throughout the Bible as a powerful message from God, offering encouragement to His chosen ones, including

---

[29] Then the Lord came down in a pillar of cloud and stood at the entrance of the tent; and He called Aaron and Miriam. When they had both come forward, [6] He said, "Now hear My words: If there is a prophet among you, I, the Lord, will make Myself known to him in a vision. I will speak with him in a dream.

[30] And the Lord appeared in the tent in a pillar of cloud, and the pillar of cloud stood at the entrance of the tent.

Abraham, Jacob, Moses, and Daniel (Genesis 15:1[31]; Numbers 21:34[32]).

In 1 Samuel 25:1, there are two encounters mentioned. The first is Saul's encounter with the medium of Endor who tells him about the death and burial of Samuel. The second is in 1 Samuel 28:9, where Saul had put the mediums and the diviners out of the land.

Similarly, King Saul is presented disguise and under the cover of night in a defeated and humiliating state as he comes to consult with the medium to find out his fate (1 Samuel 28:6, 15).

Now that Yael has Sisera, the Canaanite Army General, in her presence, she must find a way to destroy him. In 1 Samuel 28, a medium raises the spirit of the deceased Samuel during a *trance* and tells Saul of his imminent defeat and death in the war that will take place soon after this encounter.

Yael caused the ultimate destruction of the Canaanite army (Judges 4:16). This sudden action reinforces the impression that Yael is being controlled by someone orchestrating the events in her tent. First of all, she wasn't expecting any

---

[31] After these things the word of the Lord came to Abram in a vision, saying, "Do not fear, Abram, I am a shield to you; Your reward shall be very great."

[32] But the Lord said to Moses, "Do not fear him, for I have handed him over to you, and all his people and his land; and you shall do to him as you did to Sihon, king of the Amorites, who lived in Heshbon."

visitors, secondly to go from not expecting visitors to turn into an assassin leaves much to wonder.

Considering that *God is in control* and had given the prophecy to Deborah there's a possibility that divine intervention played a role in Yael's actions. Although there is no mention of a meeting between Deborah and Yael in Judges chapters 4 and 5, Deborah's prophecy about God delivering Sisera into the hands of a woman may suggest that Yael was guided by a Divine Messenger during the pivotal moment when Sisera enters in the tent. The tent of meeting where God appears and speaks to you.

God did not want people to put their faith in mediums or diviners because He preferred that they trust Him. After all, even the Mediums are accountable to God.

Jacqueline Torres

NOTES

CHAPTER SEVEN

SONG OF VICTORY

Judges 5:1-31 ~ Song of Deborah and Barak

¹ Then Deborah and Barak the son of Abinoam sang on that day, saying,

² "For the leaders leading in Israel,
For the people volunteering,
Bless the LORD!
³ Hear, you kings; listen, you dignitaries!
I myself—to the LORD, I myself will sing,
I will sing praise to the LORD, the God of Israel!
⁴ LORD, when You went out from Seir,
When You marched from the field of Edom,
The earth quaked, the heavens also dripped,
The clouds also dripped water.
⁵ The mountains flowed *with water* at the presence of
the LORD,
This Sinai, at the presence of the LORD, the God of Israel.

⁶ "In the days of Shamgar the son of Anath,
In the days of Jael, the roads were deserted,
And travelers went by roundabout ways.
⁷ The peasantry came to an end, they came to an end in
Israel,
Until I, Deborah, arose,
Until I arose, a mother in Israel.
⁸ New gods were chosen;
Then war *was in* the gates.
Not a shield or a spear was seen

Among forty thousand in Israel.
⁹ My heart *goes out* to the commanders of Israel,
The volunteers among the people;
Bless the LORD!
¹⁰ You who ride on white donkeys,
You who sit on *rich* carpets,
And you who travel on the road—shout in praise!
¹¹ At the sound of those who distribute *water* among the
watering places,
There they will recount the righteous deeds of the LORD,
The righteous deeds for His peasantry in Israel.
Then the people of the LORD went down to the gates.

¹² "Awake, awake, Deborah;
Awake, awake, sing a song!
Arise, Barak, and lead away your captives, son of Abinoam.
¹³ Then survivors came down to the nobles;
The people of the LORD came down to me as warriors.
¹⁴ From Ephraim those whose root is in Amalek *came
down*,
Following you, Benjamin, with your peoples;
From Machir commanders came down,
And from Zebulun those who wield the staff of office.
¹⁵ And the princes of Issachar *were* with Deborah;
As *was* Issachar, so *was* Barak;
Into the valley they rushed at his heels;
Among the divisions of Reuben
There were great determinations of heart.
¹⁶ Why did you sit among the sheepfolds,
To hear the piping for the flocks?
Among the divisions of Reuben
There were great searchings of heart.
¹⁷ Gilead remained across the Jordan;
And why did Dan stay on ships?

Asher sat at the seashore,
And remained by its landings.
[18] Zebulun *was* a people who risked their lives,
And Naphtali *too*, on the high places of the field.

[19] "The kings came *and* fought;
Then the kings of Canaan fought
At Taanach near the waters of Megiddo;
They took no plunder in silver.
[20] The stars fought from heaven,
From their paths they fought against Sisera.
[21] The torrent of Kishon swept them away,
The ancient torrent, the torrent Kishon.
My soul, march on with strength!
[22] Then the horses' hoofs beat
From the galloping, the galloping of his mighty stallions.
[23] 'Curse Meroz,' said the angel of the LORD,
'Utterly curse its inhabitants,
Because they did not come to the help of the LORD,
To the help of the LORD against the warriors.'

[24] "Most blessed of women is Jael,
The wife of Heber the Kenite;
Most blessed is she of women in the tent.
[25] He asked for water, she gave him milk;
In a magnificent bowl she brought him curds.
[26] She reached out her hand for the tent peg,
And her right hand for the workmen's hammer.
Then she struck Sisera, she smashed his head;
And she shattered and pierced his temple.
[27] Between her feet he bowed, he fell, he lay;
Between her feet he bowed, he fell;
Where he bowed, there he fell dead.

[28] "Out of the window she looked and wailed,
The mother of Sisera through the lattice,
'Why does his chariot delay in coming?
Why do the hoofbeats of his chariots delay?'
[29] Her wise princesses would answer her,
Indeed she repeats her words to herself,
[30] 'Are they not finding, are they not dividing the spoils?
A concubine, two concubines for every warrior;
To Sisera a spoil of dyed cloth,
A spoil of dyed cloth embroidered,
Dyed cloth of double embroidery on the neck of the
plunderer?'
[31] May all Your enemies perish in this way, LORD;
But may those who love Him be like the rising of the sun in
its might."

And the land was at rest for forty years.

When God says, "Assemble," you assemble! Believing oneself superior to the task at hand is unwise, as there are no rewards for pride and unbelief.

Jacqueline Torres

NOTES

CHAPTER EIGHT

UNSELFISH LOVE. UNCONDITIONAL MERCY.

What were the lessons learned?

As with all the Judges and other figures in Scripture, reading about their actions provides insight into ourselves. Their successes, failures, mistakes, and decisions help us learn more about our nature and God's infinite mercy and grace.

In Hebrews 11, only four of the twelve judges are listed in what is known as the Hall of Faith: Gideon, Barak, Samson, and Jephthah. Despite their selfish and disobedient actions, they were praised because of their faith.

The life of Othniel teaches important lessons about the influence of family, the role of the Holy Spirit in empowering a person's life, and the value of godly leadership in maintaining peace within a community.

The story of Ehud offers insight into how God can change the course of a nation in response to the cries of His people. It also demonstrates God's faithfulness to His promise to help Israel when they repent and turn to Him. This lesson is still relevant today.

Although Shamgar is a figure surrounded by mystery, his importance cannot be overlooked. He played a crucial role during the transitional period between the leadership of Ehud and Deborah. God used one man with one simple weapon to rescue His people from oppression. This example of God working through one person to change the lives of many applies today. We are each called to live for God, knowing that our actions can have tremendous influence over many people. Further, God often chooses to use unknown people to accomplish great achievements to bring glory to His name.

Irrespective of gender, confidence, or physical ability, all individuals can find strength when they are moved by God's Spirit and filled with His power. Additionally, Deborah serves as an example of God's tender care for His people, as she led and nurtured Israel with the same care as a mother for her children. Regardless of the instrument God chooses to use, Deborah is a biblical figure who exemplifies the power of God.

Deborah was the only woman judge in Israel. Some commentators have suggested that her appointment as judge was a rebuke to the weak-willed men of Israel. What matters most is that God chose a woman for the job because the men were unfit to judge, partly to shame them for not taking leadership. In Judges 5:6-7, Deborah describes the hardship of living under Jabin and Sisera, explaining that the highways were abandoned and travelers kept to the byways. The Israeli villages were deserted due to the danger of travel. Deborah delivers a message from God to Barak, informing him that he will lead the revolt against Sisera, who is feared by all, including Barak. Deborah agrees to accompany Barak but prophesies that a woman, not Barak, will receive the honor for the victory.

Although neither Deborah nor Yael made it to the *Hall of Faith* in Hebrews 11, they had an honored place in history as two women heroes. We learned that together, when men and women work and lead side by side, the full image of God is more profoundly expressed and God is glorified.

Women are equally capable as men in performing any task, and sometimes even better. They have been breaking down gender barriers in male-dominated roles for decades, and it is time to celebrate their achievements. Let's remember to acknowledge the importance of having women in all professions and value the unique perspective they bring to the table.

Sometimes women are better suited to certain jobs than men. This is not to say that men are inferior, but rather that certain roles require skills and qualities that are traditionally associated with women. By recognizing and celebrating women's contributions in male-dominated roles, we can create a more inclusive and diverse place in the world that benefits everyone.

In many cases, women possess the skills and qualities necessary to excel in jobs that have traditionally been associated with men. These roles often require a high level of resilience, adaptability, and emotional intelligence, which are traits commonly found in women.

Women can facilitate change and succeed in traditionally male-dominated roles and the embrace of diversity creates a culture that values all perspectives and breaks down gender barriers to success.

Deborah was a deliverer chosen by God to empower her people in a war of liberation. During her reign as judge, her people enjoyed 40 years of peace. Despite patriarchal norms, Deborah's wisdom and spirit-filled leadership prevailed. She was also referred to as a *flaming torch* because she held up the truth.

In Judges 5:6, Yael is celebrated for her heroic actions. Like Moses, who had a staff, Yael used what she had, a hammer and a peg to overcome the fear and shame brought by Sisera.

Yael's bravery serves as a reminder that we must do what we can with the resources available to us and remain watchful for opportunities that God gives us. We must remember today to celebrate women for their courage and their contributions to society. A monument should be erected to honor and commemorate their heroine achievements.

It is important to note that Yael's actions are often viewed as violent, while the violence women suffer around the world at the hands of men is frequently disregarded.

The verdict in Yael's case is multifaceted because of the effectiveness of her actions coupled with divine intervention, Sisera's status as an enemy, and his guilt for asking Yael to lie for him while he was on the run and should not have been alive. Sisera was still asserting his authority and demanding attention in someone else's territory because he was a man who thought he was still in control. *Sisera, your fate is sealed in the eyes of God*. He remembers you, and judgment will come.

Yael is a variation of the traditional motive of the woman hiding warriors, found in the stories of Rahab (Joshua 2) and the woman hiding Jonathan and Ahimaaz (2 Samuel 17:17-20[33]).

---

[33] Now Jonathan and Ahimaaz were staying at En-rogel, and a female servant would go and inform them, and they would go and inform King David, for they could not allow themselves to be seen entering the city. [18] But a boy did see them, and he told Absalom; so the two of them left quickly and came to the house of a man in Bahurim, who had a well in his courtyard, and they went down into it. [19] And the woman took a cover and spread it over the well's mouth and scattered barley meal on it, so that nothing was known. [20] Then Absalom's servants came to the woman at the house and said, "Where are Ahimaaz and Jonathan?" And

Those who take action are stepping out of the shadows and into the moment of their destiny. God was present in Yael's tent before, during, and after everything was said and done. Throughout every phase of Yael's journey, divine presence guided her steps, revealing a purpose beyond her understanding. She was living out Galatians 4:4, which refers to the moment when the fullness of time has come for the goal, the pursuit, and the transformation to be fulfilled.

Yael fulfilled her duty as part of a larger mission to stop Sisera, who had oppressed God's people for twenty years. Deborah and Yael acted as champions and warriors because men had neglected their duty. Unfortunately, women are often judged based on their gender rather than their abilities, while men's actions towards women are often ignored.

Deborah was recognized for her power, authority, and effectiveness. Her example refuted the notion that women were incapable of governing. She demonstrated a blend of authority and grace that made her a renowned and prophetic figure.

The Bible celebrates Deborah as a role model for modern women, inspiring them to be commanding and intelligent without sacrificing their femininity. Deborah embodies

---

the woman said to them, "They have crossed the brook of water." And when they searched and did not find them, they returned to Jerusalem.

confidence and authority while maintaining feminine qualities such as grace, godliness, and humility.

She was praised for her meekness as well as her ambitious goals of social and religious reform. Despite being a wife, Deborah was not limited to domestic duties; she was also a prophetess, refuting the notion that her role was solely or should only be domestic. Women in certain regions may face obstacles in holding positions of authority and knowledge, which could make it challenging for Deborah's female successors to follow in her footsteps. Nonetheless, it is achievable with God's divine guidance and purpose.

Deborah's history requires no defense or argument to convince adversaries that women should be treated with equal respect as men because God sanctions such inequality behavior in the Bible. Women should be confident in their abilities and courageous in serving God in whatever role they find themselves. It is crucial to recognize that both men and women can be used by God to perform their duties according to His will. Therefore, it is important to avoid any belief that contradicts this principle.

It is also noteworthy to mention that the pulpit fails to awaken women from the indifference of the times in inspiring them to achieve greatness, both intellectually and spiritually, in authentic fellowship with the Holy Spirit. Deborah's heroic virtues should inspire women to imitate her even though sermons rarely mention her as an example.

Yael is a heroine for slaying Sisera with only *a nail and a hammer*. Her story reminds us to use our talents to fulfill God's mission and not to question His ways because He will still move forward with you, or without you. Yael's story highlights the power of women in the Bible and her name has become synonymous with courage and female virtue in a culture that values women's roles in life. Yael is a positive model of resistance against oppressive patriarchal structures. Wearing her spiritual warrior helmet and armor, she suppressed her natural feminine emotions to fulfill her duty of killing Sisera. To successfully combat the devil and his army, one must emulate Yael and conquer your own Sisera.

Yael's decision to play the part of a patriarchal figure and her actions were guided by divine power and prophecy, and she believed they would help win the battle against Israel's enemies. It is imperative to recognize that she is exempt from judgment because she did not kill someone during a period of peace. She killed Sisera during a period of war against Israel.

Yael, a little-known nomadic warrior from a priestly clan, is honored as blessed among women, despite oppressive cultural norms for women, she courageously helped save the Israelite nation and chose to support God's people over her reputation.

Yael was married to a military businessman but remained faithful to the nation of Israel and God. She championed women's rights by eliminating the threat of sanctioned rape under the guise of *hospitality*. In the Hebrew Bible, Deborah sings her first song dedicated to Yael, who is praised for her physical strength, faithfulness, patience, and discernment.

Yael is a woman who rose from obscurity to greatness and is now synonymous with other well-known tent dwellers such as Sarah, Hagar, Leah, and Rachel. Without her remarkable act of courage, the descendants of Israel would still be suffering oppression. It is not clear whether or not God played a role in what she did or whether He was in the tent. However, one fact remains certain: it was because of Yael's bravery that Israel experienced a period of peace lasting 40 years!

Deborah is leading her people to their deliverance and she celebrates Yael's bravery in killing Sisera. In contrast, Sisera's mother imagines her son has taken Jewish girls captive and refers to other women as objects to be divided among the men who violated them. *Sisera won't be coming home, Mother!*

Although God may not always approve of our prayers, He still answers them. However, we must be careful not to pray against His command which is to pray for our enemies. God is attentive to the cries of the poor who have no protector or avenger on earth. This is especially true if the oppressed endure their suffering patiently because God will send a deliverer!

Other interpretations, however, depict Deborah in a more negative light, suggesting that she was boastful in calling herself *mother of Israel* and too proud in standing haughtily over a man.

If that were true, they would be disregarding the fact that it was Barak who willingly relinquished his leadership to her or downplaying the role of God in guiding the process.

There is a tradition that presents Deborah as being guilty of the sin of pride, which led to her loss of the gift of prophecy, while the other traditions speak in her praise, and number her among the other Israelite women for their outstanding righteousness.

Other commentators focus on Deborah's sin of pride in the Bible. Consequently, the Holy Spirit departed from her, leaving her speechless (Judges 5:7). Could it have been that they did not need prophecy for 40 years?

One of the main challenges for the rabbis was how a woman could hold a position of leadership, especially since such positions were traditionally held by men in society. Deborah positioned herself under a palm tree to be able to execute her function as judge and to avoid violating modesty laws that prohibited a woman from being alone in a room with a man who was not her husband. This ensured that she could judge the cases of the people without compromising her integrity.

Once again man putting women down! In my opinion, Deborah prioritized obedience to God's law over criticism of her leadership position, singing a victory song after the battle, or being called the mother of Israel. Why not focus on what she did when God prophesied that she was to lead Barak and his army to war with Jabin, the king of Hazor, who had oppressed the Israelites for twenty years? The Biblical account of Deborah ends with the statement that after the battle, there was peace in the land for 40 years (Judges 5:31). Thank you, Deborah and Yael!

Whether Deborah is a good example for women or not is a contentious issue in Christian interpretation. While some claim that she defies the expectation that women in traditional gender roles are to be submissive, others argue that her power exemplifies matriarchal virtue.

There were also those who were concerned about having a woman in a position of authority over Israel. You don't think it was the men who were concerned, do you? In their minds, the two prophetesses Deborah and Huldah were overly proud. They couldn't believe that Deborah summoned Barak when she should have bowed to him, and

Huldah didn't even address King Josiah as the *king*, but referred to him as the *man* instead of the king (2 Kings 22:14-15[34]).

Yael also receives mixed reviews from the rabbis. The Talmud cites the case of Yael as evidence that an act that transgresses the law, but is carried out with good intentions, is as righteous as an act that obeys the law; yet with ulterior motives. For this reason, Yael, the most blessed of women (Judges 5:24), is as praiseworthy as the matriarchs of Israel.

Yael, a heroic figure, faces moral criticism for breaching the hospitality norms of her time. But is hospitality for a fugitive general more important than the safety of a woman at risk of being raped? Be that as it may, it is crucial to remember that she was chosen as an instrument of justice in God's world, and her actions were necessary to fulfill that role.

Yael offered Sisera hospitality and protection, giving him milk to help him sleep and covering him to conceal his presence. However, we should shift our focus from the hospitality aspect and instead consider the peace of the

---

[34] So Hilkiah the priest, Ahikam, Achbor, Shaphan, and Asaiah went to Huldah the prophetess, the wife of Shallum the son of Tikvah, the son of Harhas, keeper of the wardrobe (and she lived in Jerusalem in the Second Quarter); and they spoke to her. [15] Then she said to them, "This is what the Lord, the God of Israel says: Tell the man who sent you to Me.

Israelites, who have been oppressed by Sisera for twenty years.

Yael, a virtuous woman, shows courageous loyalty to the Israelites and is celebrated as a national heroine, but is also seen as a threatening figure to men due to her actions. If Yael is an assassin with questionable morals, then it can be argued that God is responsible for *ordering the hit*, because Yael's killing of Sisera was on the same day that God granted victory to the Israelites in the defeat of the Canaanites. According to the prophecy, God is the only person in charge of all the acts in this scene.

During those days' people were doing what was right in their own eyes. The cycle of suffering, repentance, and deliverance (Judges 2:10-19), illustrates how often severe suffering will drive a person to seek God. These were wild and chaotic times in both a military and moral sense.

The people cry again, put away the foreign gods, and worship the one true God and He takes notice. After a while, even God gets tired of naming the sin. God cries out from His mercy seat. At the people's cry for help, God asks why, after being so often rescued, they keep forsaking him for other gods, why not cry to them?

To some extent, Deborah and Yael have often been at the center of disputes about the ability of women to hold positions of leadership in the church and the political sphere.

Although many suggested that Deborah's leadership as a woman was an exception that proves the rule that her story was told to encourage future women letting them know that they too could lead, as any man. They need not feel disadvantaged because of their gender because Deborah proved that women do not need the help of men, since she, not at all restrained by the weakness of her gender, undertook to perform the duties of a man, and did even more than she had undertaken. Deborah was a woman who governed the people, led armies, selected generals, and triumphed in war, that was her resume.

Deborah's credentials were *I hear what you are saying, but I am a friend of God!* In my opinion, she saw a need and she fulfilled it! God wants to know if you are willing to play any part in His mission and history, and be mindful because they are not always going to be pretty or morally correct!

The lesson to be learned is that theology and politics are intertwined, whether we acknowledge it or not. God uses flawed individuals and finds positive qualities in them, just as in the heroes of Scripture.

It is important to trust in God's plan and not question His ways when He is preparing to use you. Disobedience may lead to being offered as a sacrificial offering. Therefore, it is best to obey. Yael's actions were attributed to the Holy Spirit. It is suggested that she was in a tent when a fugitive general interrupted her history, having escaped from the battlefield where he was supposed to have died. She followed guidance with decisiveness and deserves praise. It is important to remember that success stories may not provide the full picture allowing us to speculate and use critical thinking about what was happening.

God is at work and is going ahead of you, setting up the system for you to show up in the ministry. Women and men have equal value in the Kingdom of God. God made use of wicked men and wicked nations to fulfill His purposes.

When in the presence of God, humans will experience both dread and wonder. It is only after comparing themselves to God's majesty that humans can truly appreciate their lowly state and the greatness of God. Scripture recalls that angels keep vigil for our safety, defend us, and direct our ways as they dispense and administer God's benefits (Judges 13).

The biblical account of Yael, as narrated in Judges 5:24-31, is an example of the courageous and unwavering spirit of women who are anointed by God. These women, imbued with the divine spirit, are not weak, but are rather motivated, inspiring, and leaders among their fellow women and leaders alike.

God, the supreme commander of all battles, has a special place in His heart for those whom he deems worthy of His greatest challenges. These challenges are not always easy, but they are always worth the effort, and they are often the source of great triumphs.

In fact, women of God should take courage from the example set by Yael, who was unwavering in her resolve despite the daunting task that she faced.

In Christianity, Jesus of Nazareth is considered the true Messiah and the judge of Israel. Despite the efforts of all twelve tribes, no one was able to remain faithful enough to bring permanent glory to God. Therefore, God sent Jesus to finish the task once and for all. As believers, it is our responsibility to continue the legacy of Jesus until His return.

Yael, the warrior woman, motivates, leads and inspires women. God endows women with a warrior disposition. God is sending His best soldiers into the great wars. The days of victory are at hand. Godly women, rise up. God knows what He has placed in you. Ladies, endowed with a heavenly anointing!

Deborah as well as Barak sang spiritual Songs of Victory to God, so did Miriam and Moses. What is your Song of Victory? How did you fight your enemy? Do you know your enemy by name? How long has your enemy been oppressing you?

MEET THE AUTHOR

Dr. Jacqueline Torres is the author of numerous books both written in English and Spanish. Her latest publication, Yael: ¡Una Mujer, un Clavo, un Martillo! Her areas of interest include writing non-fiction stories and personal development.

She received her PhD of Philosophy in Theology and Licensing in Pastoral Ministry. She is an executive business leader with multifaceted experience in non-profits and governmental agencies. With her entrepreneurial spirit, she founded several organizations and coached other leaders to establish their businesses.

She has experience as a producer, host of radio programs, and civic journalist. She has received numerous awards from government/non-governmental agencies for her contributions to addressing community issues, including business and religion. In addition to her professional experience as a writer, she has worked as an adjunct professor and educator. Currently, she serves as a psychoeducator within a clinical setting for male parolees and probationers, facilitating groups, providing evaluation, counseling, preventive action, and preventive rehabilitation to men who have difficulty adjusting socially after incarceration.

Dr. Torres does not take any issue she writes about lightly, and because of her professional decorum, she ensures that she conducts thorough research to present her best when writing for her readers and followers.

A curious peculiarity of her is that she loves her manuscripts and clings to them very tightly and the only way she can let them go is by going to the beach, giving them one last look, releasing them metaphorically with the waves and then sending them to the printers.

She has been invited as a keynote speaker at conferences, retreats, workshops, panels and other national platforms.

For your next event and learn more about her you can visit www.authorjacquelinetorres.com or drjacquelinetorres@cox.net

PORTFOLIO

Success is always evolving. Your success is unique to you. Your success is not going to look like anyone else's. Your success is going to have your own glow!

Upon meeting the author, one encounters a person who is not merely an advocate for the advancement of others, but rather a proponent of equal opportunity and access for all. Jacqueline Torres is a woman of considerable influence and experience, who has overcome significant challenges in her life. Despite these obstacles, she has succeeded in achieving her goals. —She Made It!

In her spare time, she teaches other writers how to create a manuscript. During her book tours, she meets numerous individuals who have written numerous pieces but lack knowledge about the initial steps of publishing a book. She has coached many writers to publish their first book, is constantly in demand for speaking engagements, and best of all, she speaks two languages, English and Spanish.

She is an imaginative, inquisitive writer who loves to tell stories. Her passion with the ability of words to uplift, educate, and amuse people has led her to focus her professional life on telling gripping tales that genuinely engage her audience.

Her partnership with Manuscritos Publishing, which led to Manuscritos Publishing being chosen as the Community Champion by Citizens Bank, is one of her numerous values. Her efforts to close disparities in the general community, with a focus on the Latino population specifically, were acknowledged with this honor.
www.manuscritospublishing.com

Dr. Torres is also a creative graphic designer. She has an online print-on-demand store, called LibrosBOOKtique, which offers a variety of products, including stickers, t-shirts, and other accessories, featuring the covers of her books. Over 1200 designs to shop from the comfort of your seat! Shop Now and Save 20%!
https://rdbl.co/3hoVNBK

She is consistently seeking novel avenues to disseminate her creative expertise. Her inaugural children's Christmas coloring book, comprising 94 pages of festive and loving content, is a testament to her ingenuity. You can find it in Amazon https://a.co/d/eWWVZJP

She is the presenter and founder of the program: ¡Mujer Resucita! and ¡Mujer, Recibe Tu Unción! A social series of topics for women which include personal, professional, spiritual, family, friendships, relationships, business, health, food, and the future. For information or to register today go to uncionmujer@gmail.com or visit
https://mujerrecibetuuncion.com/

Yael: She Nailed Him!

BIBLIOGRAPHY

Boer, Roland, ed. (2013). Postcolonialism and the Hebrew Bible: the next step. Society of Biblical Literature.

Brenner, Athalya and Yee, Gale A. eds. (2013). Joshua and Judges. Fortress Press Publishing.

Brenner-Idan, Athalya. (2015). The Israelite Woman: social role and literary type in biblical narrative. Bloomsbury Publishing.

Carol A. Newsom, Ringe, Sharon H., Lapsley, Jacqueline E. eds. (2012). Women's Bible Commentary, Third Edition. Westminster John Knox Press.

Conway, Colleen M. (2017). Sex and Slaughter in the Tent of Yael: a cultural history of a biblical story. Oxford University Press.

Frymer-Kensky, Tikva. (2002). Reading the Women of the Bible. Schocken Books.

Garcia Bachmann, Mercedes L. (2018). Pilarski-Calderon, Ahida, Reid, Barbara E., eds. Judges Wisdom Commentary. Liturgical Press Publishing.

Gunn, David M. (2005). Judges through the Centuries. Wiley Blackwell Publishing.

Hollyday, Joyce. (1994). Clothed with the Sun: biblical women, social justice, and us. Westminster John Knox Publishing.

Nelson, Richard D. (2017). Judges: A Critical and Rhetorical Commentary. Bloomsbury T&T Clark Publishing.

Niditch, Susan. (2008). Judges: Commentary. Westminster John Knox Publishing.

Salkin, Jeffrey K. (2008). Righteous Gentiles in the Hebrew Bible: ancient role models for sacred relationships. Jewish Lights Publishing.

Taylor, Marion Ann, De Groot, Christiana, eds. (2016). Women of War, Women of Woe: Joshua and Judges through the Eyes of Nineteenth-century Female Biblical Interpreters. William B. Eerdmans Publishing.

Biblical References

Biblegateway.com (*all scripture references are New American Standard Bible ~ NASB unless otherwise mentioned*.)

God was responsible.

God granted the victory.

God was the only person in charge!

www.ingramcontent.com/pod-product-compliance
Lightning Source LLC
Chambersburg PA
CBHW070816100426
42742CB00012B/2376